Miranda's Shadow

short stories

Kitty Fitzgerald, Irish writer, lives on the North East Coast of
England. Her other work includes four novels:
Marge (Sheba 1985), *Snapdragons* (Brandon 1999),
Small Acts of Treachery (Brandon 2002), *Pigtopia* (Faber
2005), which took second place in the Barnes & Noble
Discover New Writers Awards (fiction) 2006.
She has had eight theatre plays produced, most recently,
Making Plans for Jessica (2011, Anne Orwin's Youth
Theatre) and *Bingo!* (2010, Cloud Nine Theatre).
Four of her radio dramas have been produced by BBC Radio 4.
Kitty has edited three anthologies of short fiction for IRON
Press, most recently, *ROOT*, stories by North East
Writers, 2013.

First published 2013 by IRON Press
5 Marden Terrace
Cullercoats
North Shields
NE30 4PD
T: +44 (0)191 2531901
E: ironpress@blueyonder.co.uk
www.ironpress.co.uk

ISBN 978-0-9565725-9-2

Printed by Fieldprint Ltd
Boldon on Tyne

IRON Press Books are distributed by Central Books
and represented by Inpress Books Ltd
Churchill House, 12 Moseley St
Newcastle upon Tyne, NE1 1DE
T: +44 (0) 191 2308104
www.inpressbooks.co.uk

Supported using public funding by
ARTS COUNCIL
ENGLAND
LOTTERY FUNDED

Miranda's Shadow
short stories

Kitty Fitzgerald

IRON
PRESS

Acknowledgements are made to the
Hosking Houses Trust
for their residency (Sept-Dec 2012)
and financial support.
www.hoskinghouses.co.uk

Thanks also to, The Authors' Foundation
and The Society of Authors.
Kitty was the recipient of: a Hawthornden
Fellowship in 2005,
a Time to Write Award, Arts Council
England 2003 and
The C P Taylor Playwriting Bursary 2002

Her story, *The Bones of Saint Ignatious* won
the 2009 Latitude Festival/Notes from The
Underground Short Story Competition.
The story, *Miranda's Shadow* was first published,
2012, in *Platform*, New Fiction by North East Writers,
commissioned by New Writing North 2012.
Once Were Angels Here was first published
online by Shortfire Press, 2011.
www.shortfirepress.com

Contents

In memory of Joseph & Mary Fitzgerald
and Khodor Dannan

Miranda's Shadow

THERE'S SOMETHING ABOUT SHADOWS. HAVE YOU NOTICED? They have substance but it's different from ours. It comes from another place, someplace concurrent but shifty, shifting. I found that out when I was at junior school. There was a girl in my class, an unusual girl, called Miranda. She was the most beautiful thing I'd ever seen with her bright burgundy hair and lilac eyes. She had some syndrome or other, can't remember what it was called, but she rarely made eye contact and seldom spoke.

One day, in the playground, a group of us were having a game of chase and I ended up quite close to Miranda, in the corner of the yard where she always retreated from the rest of us. It was a brilliant day, robin's egg sky, not a sliver of a breeze. I don't know why but I looked down at her shadow, facing away from me, just like her. And as I continued to stare, it turned, trembled and started moving away from her body towards mine. I was terrified. Miranda saw my fear, I'm certain of that because she looked at me. For the first time in the eight years she'd been at the school, she actually looked directly at me for more than one second.

That was the starting point for my fascination with shadows. I wanted to know everything about them, like where they came from. I mean, were they there at birth? Mam was pregnant with my sister Charlie at the

Leabharlanna Fhine Gall

time and I told her I wanted to be present at the birth. She refused, said I was too young and did a lot of tut-tutting. I couldn't let it go though. I needed to know if a new born baby had a shadow. So I wore her down by doing loads of internet research and found dozens of reasons why I should be present at the birth.

One, I could help with her breathing exercises; dad was useless at stuff like that. Two, we were doing a project on childbirth at school (lie). Three, I might not bond with my sister if I wasn't present at the birth...

'I said no,' Mam cut in. But with a bit of persuasion from Dad – after I promised to wash the car every week until the end of the month – she agreed to let me wait in the corridor and slip inside the delivery room the moment Charlie was in her arms. I have to admit to having second and third thoughts when I heard the mewling and squawking leaking out of the room. Once I got inside I was ambushed for several minutes by the gurgling, beetroot-faced bundle lying on mam's chest. Then I checked from every angle in the room, made sure the sun was coming in the window, even put on some lights. Guess what? There wasn't one. No shadow, not even a hint.

After that I haunted baby Charlie. First thing in the morning I went on the shadow hunt. After school, every day, I was straight on her case. Mam and Dad just thought I was crazy about my new sister. I could hardly tell them the truth. Want to know what I discovered? Six months old, that's when the shadow truly emerged.

It wasn't scientific, obviously; you'd have to set up a huge project and monitor thousands of babies to be able to come to any worthwhile conclusion. However, it confirmed for me what I already suspected: shadows are not integral to the body, they're separate. That's when I began obsessing. I started with my own shadow. It wasn't impressive; it was too pale, ill defined and sort of ragged at the edges. Still, it didn't wander or try to run away like others I saw. Later I discovered that often, the shadow a

person casts is quite different from the face they put out
to the world. They can appear average, conventional, pay-
your-bills-on-time, never-rock-any-boat types, but catch
their shadow on a real bright day and it can be jagged,
sharp, conflicted. And vice versa, the ones that seem laid
back, extrovert and radical, their shadows are sometimes
curiously bland.

Then there are the shadows that aren't fully
connected, like Miranda's. If they catch you staring, they
often move independently of their bodies. It's awesome. I
once saw this guy in Exhibition Park. He had two small
kids with him. It was an ultramarine sky and I could
clearly see all of their shadows. At first they seemed fine
but when for some reason the guy lost it and started
bellowing and ranting, the kids' shadows began to shrink
and started looking about, as if they wanted to escape. At
the same time, the man's began to grow until it was
massive and surrounded the children's. I was frightened
and at the same time, intrigued by what was happening; I
couldn't turn away, it was invaluable research. But when
the man saw me watching, he shouted,

'What 're ye looking at?' And his shadow began
to leak towards mine, smoothly, like demented lubricant.
I ran away, fast.

My whole life has been a research project. I'm
twenty-seven and I run a science fiction book and film
shop in Newcastle called *Shadowlands* where I keep a
record of all things shady. Hey, remember that fantastic,
surprising scene in the film, *The Third Man*? When the
light comes on in the window and shows the Harry Lime
character hiding in the shadow of a doorway opposite
with a cat sitting on his shoes? That's class. I think Carol
Reed knew about shadows. What about the strange small
boy with the rubber ball who suddenly cast a huge
shadow as he led the mob after Holly Martins? Was it
distortion or was it real? And later, when Martins was
being questioned about seeing Harry Lime, who was
supposed to be dead, he actually said,

'I was chasing his shadow.' Did he mean that Lime's shadow was separate from his body? Was Carol Reed actually trying to warn us about shadows?

Coppola definitely knows. He showed it in his version of *Dracula*, the way a shadow can move independently of its owner. If it gave you the shivers watching the film, imagine what it's like to witness it happening in real time. And it's not the sort of thing you can drop into a conversation is it? Hey, do you know the truth about shadows? That's probably why I'm a loner. I'm not happy about getting close to other people's shadows. You just never know.

Anyway, after I saw Coppola's *Dracula* for the tenth time, I got to thinking about Miranda, about the way her shadow had moved towards me that day in the school playground and started this whole obsession off. And I knew I had to find her and see her shadow one more time.

The internet's a wonderful thing, if you know how to use it, and I do. It took me less than half an hour to trace her. I was surprised to discover that she was lecturing in art at Northumbria University. Because of the way she'd behaved at school I'd expected her to be in some sort of care facility or still living with her parents. Her phone number was right there in the regular directory.

When I rang she repeated my name with a question mark, 'Callum Delaney?'

'I'm sorry, you probably don't remember me—' I began.

'Yes, I do,' she said. 'Callum, the maths genius with the licorice hair. I'm just surprised because I was thinking about you last week, wondering what had happened to you.'

'Synchronicity,' I said.

'Strange,' she replied. 'Are you still a bit spooky?'

'Me? I thought it was you that was weird.'

'No, I was withdrawn, with a touch of Asperger's.

You were nutty. The way you could do all that mental arithmetic, didn't you realize it freaked everybody out?'

'You hardly ever spoke,' I retaliated.

'Nobody else could get a word in when you were around.'

She laughed and I suddenly remembered hearing that sound in class one day when I got ten out ten, yet again, for the maths test; it was like wooden chimes rippling in the wind.

'What are you up to Callum, still solving complex geometrical problems?'

'Running a science fiction film and bookshop called *Shadowlands.*'

'Mmm, that figures.'

When I suggested meeting up she seemed positively eager. We agreed to have a coffee the following day.

'Promise you won't talk algebra all the time?'

'I promise.'

I stayed late at work, checking in the new stock, and clearing out the old to take to charity shops. My future meeting with Miranda lingered in my mind the whole time. The strangest thing about it was how relaxed I felt.

In bed later, I read an article I'd been saving from *Nature* magazine. It was about a young woman with no history of psychiatric problems who was being checked out for epilepsy. When a certain part of her brain – the left temporoparietal junction – was electrically stimulated, she talked about how she had encounters with a 'shadow person'. I'd heard of shadow people before but I thought they were just poorly connected shadows. Perhaps I was wrong.

It was a sharp, cloudless day with a high sun. We met at the outdoor café in front of the Theatre Royal in Newcastle and I couldn't resist glancing at her shadow. It was strong, beautifully formed, no jagged edges and completely stable. She caught me looking and smiled.

'You saw it, that day in the playground, didn't you?' she said as we sat down. I was so startled that she remembered, I just gave her one of my puzzled looks. 'My shadow,' she went on. 'You saw the way my shadow moved, the way it wasn't really mine. I know you saw it. I'm so glad you got in touch.'

I came clean with her then; told her about my obsession, why I'd tracked her down, my research on my baby sister, everything. And she told me what I must have known all along,

'Sometimes people get the wrong shadows,' she said. 'The system fails, there's a glitch and a mismatch occurs. That's what happened to me.'

'How did you find out?'

'Out of the corner of my eye, I kept seeing it move and twitch as if it didn't want to be with me.' She paused as the coffee arrived.

'Who do you get in touch with about something like that?' I asked.

'I became that quiet, watchful child that you remember, until when I was thirteen, my mother got pregnant with my brother. And once when we were picking her up from an appointment at the hospital, I suddenly thought: what if someone born around the same time as me got my shadow by mistake?'

'What a brilliant idea; it could explain such a lot of the weird shadow activity I've seen.' She touched my hand and smiled.

'I went to see my doctor and told him I was doing a special study at school and needed to know how many children were born in the same hospital as me on the same day and what their names were. He was very helpful.' She dunked her croissant in her coffee and manoeuvered it into her mouth without dribbling a single drop. I was very impressed.

'And?' I asked as she finished eating.

She grinned, cat-like, before checking her watch. 'I have to get back to work, so I'll give you the quick version. My shadow was trying to live on a lad who'd been born in the same hospital as me but the day before. Unfortunately, the shadow I had didn't belong to the boy and he wouldn't listen when I tried to explain the situation to him. He was too unsettled, too angry. So, I just went very close to him. My shadow recognized me and left his body. My errant shadow had no choice but to go to the lad because my real shadow dislodged it. I'm afraid I never saw him again and often wondered what happened to him.'

I asked her to repeat it more slowly and she did. I shook my head. 'Difficult to believe, but from what I know I'm sure it's true.'

As we stood up to leave, she took my hand and turned me so that we were side by side with our backs to the sun. And there on the ground were our shadows, dark as tar: hers, lovely and strong and mine, as always, fragile and blurred at the extremes. I started to pull away but her shadow turned towards mine and merged with it for just a second. I shivered as Miranda turned and kissed me, filling up my whole body with a sort of joy.

'I never forgot you, Callum,' she said. 'Come to dinner at my place this evening.' I was so overwhelmed I couldn't speak. She wrote down her address. 'Seven-thirty at mine and bring a bottle.'

As she walked away I was already planning on taking my *The Third Man* DVD with me. When I glanced at my shadow again, it had changed. It was rich, clearly defined, deeply embedded in the earth and in me.

The Knowledge

ONE YEAR WHEN THE CROPS WERE POOR MY GRANDDAD DUG UP
the fairy mound in the far west pasture to make use of the
land for extra planting. It was a desperate act. Up in the
attic for three evenings we'd heard the arguments rising
up from the big kitchen below, going back and forth
between him and Grandma.

'You can't turn your back on six generations of
family. They've honoured the agreement never to touch
the mound,' she said.

'It's just superstition, Ruth,' he said.

'Your father wasn't a superstitious man, but he
kept the promise.'

Peeping through the slats at the top of the
staircase we saw Granddad swipe his hand up his face
and over his hair, as if he could wipe away Grandma's
resistance. The fire cracked in the grate, spitting resin,
almost like a warning.

'We've barely enough food for the animals and if
we don't feed them we'll be without milk, cheese, eggs, let
alone meat. I have no choice,' he said finally.

Out of the attic window we watched him stride
over the near pastures towards the disputed mound, a
large shovel propped on his shoulder. It was almost dusk
but he had to go while he had the resolve, so he told us
the next morning.

I was on holiday from England and staying at the house for four weeks, along with two cousins, Liam and Breda who were the children of Aunt Kate up in the Mellary Mountains. With Grandma interrupting from the back kitchen, Granddad gathered us round the old beech wood table to explain the hoo-hah we'd heard the night before.

'It's not something I do lightly, children,' he said. 'But I'm responsible for this family and I have to do what I think is best.'

'Your father will be turning in his grave,' Grandma shouted.

'My father would understand the situation. Two years of drought and failed crops has a way of sharpening the mind. That patch of land runs over the well so it's easily irrigated.'

'A promise is a promise.'

'It's a story, Ruth. It's been passed down for so many years nobody knows the real details anymore.'

'I do,' said Pat Dwyer as he marched through the open door and plonked his backside firmly in the rocking chair next to the fire. He was the churchwarden, with three sons who had gone to be priests up in Dublin and he was also Grandma's oldest brother.

Wiping her hands on a towel, Grandma strolled into the room avoiding Granddad's eyes.

'Well Pat, what's brought you here so early on a Saturday morning?' Granddad asked.

'Ah, needs must when the devil calls, James,' Dwyer replied.

'I sent for him,' Grandma admitted and I flushed up, being the culprit who had carried the message between the two of them. Granddad shook his head at me.

'Outside you three,' he ordered, his voice sterner than usual. We obeyed without question.

We got into the back kitchen via the outside door. Huddled together behind the pantry we strained to hear what was being said.

gة

'I hear what you're saying, Pat, but this really is my business,' Granddad said.

'A promise made to the fairies and then broken reflects on all of us that share the land. I've called the family to meet here at two-thirty on Sunday.'

Some more words were exchanged but they were too quiet for us to catch. We skipped out into the yard and up into the depleted hayloft before Grandma caught us listening. The bales, which normally rose up to the false ceiling below the roof, stood only four feet from the ground. I suddenly understood Granddad's side of the argument.

'D'you believe in the small people?' Liam asked me.

'D'you?' I asked, not willing to commit.

'Of course we do. They've always lived in and among us.'

'Well why can't we see them then?' I asked.

'Because they don't want you to.'

'They don't trust us,' Breda chipped in.

'Sometimes they take the shape of an animal. Anyway, I asked you first. Do you believe?' Liam insisted.

'I don't know. The fairies talked and written about in England are of a different sort. And people there don't believe in things they can't see,' I replied.

'Is that why they're heathens and don't believe in God?' Breda said.

Liam pulled a wad of hay from a bale and threw it at Breda. 'You'd better wise up before you come up to the big school or they'll make mincemeat of you,' he said.

'Don't pull at the hay, Liam,' I said.

'Why ever not?'

'You heard what Granddad said about the drought and stuff.'

He pushed his face close to mine and said in a sing-song voice,

'I'll tell Grandma you're on his side.'

I wanted to slap him; instead I crawled over to

the ladder, climbed up to the false ceiling platform and gazed out over the pasture behind the house. I was an only child and used to getting my own way so I wasn't good at negotiating power with others. Down below, Liam and Breda were mumbling quietly and I was steaming with worry that they might stop being my friends.

Out of the window I watched Grandma gathering eggs from the hens into her pinafore. Pat Dwyer and her were chatting on. Then a sudden movement in the field behind her caught my eye. It was like a fragment of heat haze and then it sharpened into a fox with fur so red it hurt my eyes and forced them shut. When I blinked them open I couldn't see the fox, but I scrambled down the ladder to the bales, shouting,

'Fox, fox, there's a fox in the field near the henhouse.'

As I ran to find Grandma, Breda and Liam joined me, all of us shouting ourselves hoarse. But we were too late. Grandma and Pat were running after the fox through the field, brandishing rakes and cursing loudly. Feathers and blood glistened on the grass. Climbing on top of the pasture wall, we saw the tail of the fox thrashing along up ahead with the dead hen slumped in its mouth.

When Grandma and Pat stopped running and turned around, Liam and Breda climbed down but I remained standing on the wall and watched as the fox headed into the far west pasture towards the fairy mound. Granddad ran up from milking the goats and caught Grandma and Pat turning back into the yard. She was bursting with fury.

'This is your fault, James,' she shouted.

He tried to fold her into his arms but she pushed him away.

'It's the fairies, James. It's retribution. Promise me you won't lay another spade in that ground.'

'Listen to her, man,' said Pat Dwyer.

Granddad sagged inwards from the middle, like someone punched in the stomach. 'I can't promise that,

Ruth,' he said quietly.

'Then I won't speak another word to you until you do.' She brushed past him, pausing only to pick up the eggs she'd left on the grass next to the log pile.

Pat Dwyer marched off and Granddad glanced at the three of us, me still standing on the wall, Liam and Breda leaning against it.

'Don't worry, it'll be all right,' he said, slowly turning to go back to return to the goats.

At thirteen I was the oldest and even though I was as miserable as the others, I took it upon myself to chivvy my cousins along.

'Let's go to the fairy mound and ask them to forgive Granddad,' I said.

Liam shook his head and Breda followed suit but I'd picked up a slight hesitation.

'We'll make a ritual of it, a procession round the mound and some chanting like at Mass. I can do a bit of the Credo in Latin,' I said.

The weariness seeped out of their faces. 'Some candles out of Grandma's box under the stairs?' Breda suggested.

'And Holy Water,' Liam said, his eyes fire-bright. 'I'll cycle down to the church and fetch some.'

'Good,' I said. 'We'll meet in the barn after dinner. Breda will get candles and matches, you the Holy Water and I'll have the words.'

Back up in the attic I rummaged my brain for Latin words and phrases from the Mass. Downstairs, Grandma clattered pans and pots as she made bread and soup. Granddad stayed working out of doors, not even returning for his tea and biscuits, which were, as usual, placed on the table exactly at eleven.

Later, around the dinner table, the adults ignored us and kept their eyes on the food. I was consumed with a missionary zeal: to make things right with the fairies, no matter what. The adrenalin rush made me dizzy. As I pushed back my chair to leave the table, Grandma spoke.

'Where do you think you're going?'

I glanced from her to Liam and Breda, struggling for the right thing to say.

'Sure we're off playing, Nana, we have the games all sorted,' Breda said.

'Not this afternoon my little peashooters,' Grandma said. 'We're off to the Nire Valley to visit Larry and Madge. They've invited you to go swimming in the river with them and have a picnic afterwards at Aunty Nellie's.'

'I'll come along with you,' Granddad said.

'Johanna, tell your grandfather that won't be necessary,' Grandma said as she left the table. 'You kids can clear the dishes into the scullery before you get washed and dressed.'

Liam, Breda and I stared at Granddad. His face was washed white with an oily sheen. He looked ill.

'You should have a rest Granddad, you don't look well,' I suggested.

He sighed like the old goat after milking. 'Perhaps you're right Johanna,' he said. 'I slept badly last night. You go off and have your fun, I'll see to the table and the washing up. And give Aunty Nellie and the twins my love.'

At dusk, when we returned, all boisterous from the Nire Valley, we found Granddad draped like an empty sack over the arm of the rocking chair. His breathing was loud and ragged. The dishes were still on the table. Grandma rushed over to him and felt his forehead and his pulse. Her eyes were wild when she turned back to us.

'Come, help me, we have to get him into bed,' she said.

It was a struggle. Grandma held under his arms, Liam and I each had a leg and Breda went ahead, opening doors and turning down the bed. While Grandma prepared a tincture, we took it in turns to wipe his face and head with cool flannels. When she carried the mug into the downstairs bedroom the whiske y smell tickled my nose.

She sent us off then, to wash, clean teeth and get our nightclothes on. As we got ready for bed, the three of us whispered our fears to each other.

'Is it the fairy curse?' Breda asked.

'More than likely,' Liam replied.

'Well then, if it is, we have to do our ritual at the mound early tomorrow, agreed?'

The two of them nodded and we went quietly down the stairs.

When we got there Grandma had Granddad's top layers off and she was examining his bare right arm. Liam gasped. When Grandma straightened up I saw that Granddad's arm was twice its normal size and covered in ugly blisters.

'Johanna,' Grandma said. 'Put a coat on over your pyjamas and get over to your Uncle Pat's. Fetch Aunty Maeve back with you. Tell her to bring mustard and some sloe gin.'

'Is it the fairies?' I heard Breda ask as I left the room.

I didn't wait for the answer. Pulling on my duffle coat, I took Liam's bike and pedalled like a mad thing all the way down Glasha and into Four Mile Water, skidding on the gravel spread thin on Uncle Pat's lane.

Maeve was putting her kids to bed. They were young and clingy.

'She'll be with you directly,' Pat said. 'Take a seat.'

I sat opposite him and he asked me to describe Granddad's arm. I did my best.

When I'd finished he sighed. ''Tis the fairies have him taken, I'm sure of it.'

Upstairs Maeve was singing a Gaelic lullaby.

'Uncle Pat?'

'Yes?'

'Tell me the story of the fairies and why the mound in the far west pasture mustn't be touched?'

He leaned his head back on the chair for a second and licked his lips.

'The Church is against these stories, Johanna. I don't want to be the one who tells you. You must ask your parents.'

'What must she ask them?' Maeve asked as she came downstairs.

'About the fairies,' I said.

'Come with me Johanna, we have to get the mustard and gin. Pat, you stay awake until I get back, you hear? We might have need of you.'

'I'll be waiting.'

With everything gathered into a basket, we set off walking back, me wheeling the bike and Maeve with her arm on my shoulder.

'Now Johanna, I'm going to tell you what Pat wouldn't because in this situation I know your mammy and daddy would want you told.' I nodded and she went on.

'Before there was the Church, people believed there were Spirits in the world.'

'I didn't know there was a time before the Church.'

'Well there was, and the Spirits were called many names like, fairies, elves, goblins and giants. Some of them lived far from humans, in wild places deep in forests or underground, and wanted nothing to do with us. Others lived close by and sometimes showed themselves. But they were not like the creatures in fairy tales. They were gifted and often dangerous, and lived in Elfhame, a world parallel to ours. Back then people feared the Spirits and never spoke badly of them because they could see into the future and could create as well as cure disease.'

'Many, many years back a boy who lived on this land of ours accidentally discovered an opening into their other world.'

'The fairy mound?' I asked.

She nodded. 'He was called Noel and for days

he'd been tracking a fox who was killing their hens.'

'A fox came and took one of Grandma's hens yesterday.'

'She would have known what it meant. So, Noel tracked the fox to the mound and saw it go underground. In those days the mound was surrounded by woodland so thick, Noel could only just squeeze through it. There, between two large rocks he saw fox markings, other strange footprints and a trail of blood and feathers.'

We were halfway up Glasha when Maeve paused. I remained silent, desperate to hear the rest.

'Instead of telling his parents, Noel fetched his younger brother, Colm, and together they carried sticks, peat and matches. Noel planned to smoke out the fox as he'd seen his father once do with a wildcat that got in among the goats.'

She paused, pulling me tightly towards her. ''Twas a tragedy, Johanna. They got the fire lit and for a short time nothing happened. Noel thought maybe he'd killed the fox until, with a noise like gunfire, the biggest stone suddenly cracked and all manner of strange creatures swarmed from out of the split stone. They scratched and tore at Noel's skin, shouting in a language unknown to him. Then two of the largest winged creatures picked up his brother Colm and flew out over the woods with him.'

We set off walking in silence. My heart was still clattering in my ears when she stopped walking, only yards from Grandma's house.

'Are you all right?' Maeve asked.

'Yes, I'm fine,' I said, though a shiver ran through me. 'Did they find Colm?'

'No, nobody ever saw him again.'

'What happened to Noel?'

'He never recovered. He became a silent, lonely man and died childless. His grandfather had bought the land very cheaply from an old woman who told him about the fairy mound, how it was a sacred place and must never be disturbed. And he'd kept it safe and passed knowledge of it to his son, Noel's father. But Noel's father had not passed the knowledge to his own child, thinking him too young to understand. After the tragedy he sold up and left the area, went back to Donegal. That's when our family came by the acres and the knowledge. And for six hundred years we have kept it safe...until now.'

The top half of the stable door into the kitchen was open. Grandma must have heard us talking. She stepped up to the road and called out,

'Hurry Maeve, I have the poultice nearly ready.'

While Grandma and Maeve got to work in the kitchen, I went into the downstairs bedroom. Liam and Breda were lying across the bed, watching Granddad's erratic breathing shift the bedclothes about. I quickly told them what Maeve had told me.

'So you see, in the morning I'll have to go alone to the mound. I can't risk one of you being taken by them.'

'I should go,' Liam said. 'I'm the male.'

His heart wasn't in it. Breda took hold of his hand but he brushed her away. 'You go Johanna', Breda said. 'You have the words and we'll give you the candles and the Holy Water tonight.'

'But if you're not back sharpish, we'll have to tell,' Liam added.

'Yes, I know.'

Maeve and Grandma arrived then. One carrying a large steaming bowl, the other long strips of material cut from a towel. Grandma spread an old sheet along the side of the bed nearest Granddad.

'What's in the bowl?' Breda asked.

'A magic poultice,' she said. 'No more questions now or you'll be up the stairs.'

Maeve laid the strips on the sheet, Grandma spread on mixture from the bowl. It was an acid yellow veined with purple. Each time she wrapped a new strip around his arm, Maeve said its number and Grandma whispered Gaelic words. Thirty-two times they did this before loudly exhaling.

'Why did you use thirty-two strips?' I asked.

'Magic numbers,' Maeve said. 'Three for optimism and two for peacemaking.'

'Off to bed with you,' Grandma said, chasing us out of the room.

In the attic we packed a little bag with candles, matches and Holy Water.

'Do you have the words learnt?' Breda asked.

I nodded, though I already knew I wouldn't say any of the Latin Mass at the mound. These were Spirits from a time before the Church and I had no words for that. Neither could I use the Holy Water. Instead, I wrote the number 32 on some paper and covered the rest of the space with my best drawings of flowers and stars. Liam set his alarm clock for six a.m.

My sleep was disturbed, punctuated by strange sounds coming from Granddad downstairs and wild images emanating from the things Maeve told me. After one ring, Liam shut off the alarm and we all got out of bed. While I was dressing, Breda tiptoed to the top of the stairs to see if Grandma was about.

'No sign of her,' she whispered.

'Good luck,' Liam said.

With the bag over my shoulder I crept down the stairs. The fire was still going in the kitchen and I took a warm of it before glancing into the downstairs bedroom. Grandma was asleep in the armchair, a rug pulled up to her throat and her head turned to one side. Granddad had stopped the loud, uneven breathing and now his chest barely rose at all. I put my hand on his head. He was on fire and out of the corner of his mouth something red dribbled down onto his chin.

In the kitchen I put on my boots and ran out into the yard, scattering the pecking hens. Over the gate I climbed and plodded quickly across the grass, which was still wet with morning dew. I kept my eyes peeled for foxes or heat haze, though the sun was barely above the horizon. My feet were heavy, my breath like an anxious dog at the vet's. I looked back at the house to see Liam and Breda's faces pressed up against the attic window.

At the threshold of the far west pasture I paused. Way behind me I thought I heard someone shouting but I didn't look back. Slowly but deliberately I approached the mound. All about its edges was evidence of felled trees and the further in I walked the colder it became. In the centre were thick lumps of grass knitted around large rocks. I walked the whole perimeter until I found the rock that Liam split. Inside its crevices something shimmered and moved.

Taking three candles out of my bag I pushed them into the ground a little distance from the rock. As I lit each one I chanted,

'Forgive him, please forgive him.'

Next I took the piece of paper with the number 32 and my drawings on. Saying the same words, I gently pushed it into the crevice. When it was halfway through it was pulled sharply from within. I gasped but carried on with my words,

'We will plant fresh trees and we will build a wall around them so everyone will know not to trespass. And we will tell the tale of the fairy mound for generations to come, of your power and your mercy. Please spare my Granddad.'

First came hissing sounds, next the pressure of tiny hands all over my head, face and arms and then the words, which sounded like they came from the throat of someone being strangled. It was a terrifying noise.

'We will take something from you,' it said, 'a trophy so that you will never forget this day.'

'What do you want?'

'Push your hand where you put the paper.'

I didn't want to do it but I knew I mustn't anger them, so slowly I slid my hand in towards the voice that chilled me...

I woke to a rhythmic motion. Grandma had me on her knee. She was rocking back and forth in front of the fire. A knitted shawl was wrapped around me.

'She's opening her eyes,' Liam shouted.

He had come after me and then fetched Connor Dolan from the next farm to help carry me to the house.

The fairies had taken the top of the little finger on my left hand. I could feel the throb of its loss through Grandma's expert bandaging. I'd got off lightly.

'You've been very lucky,' Grandma said. I saw the pain in her eyes from the knowledge of what could have happened.

Wearing his dressing gown, Granddad came in from the bedroom. Breda held his hand and guided him to the other rocking chair.

'You shouldn't be up,' Grandma said.

'I had to see my heroine, Johanna. The girl who tried to save the land from my stupidity... and besides I feel a lot better.

'Good, it's time to remove the poultice.'

Granddad nodded, took off his dressing gown and pulled up the sleeve of his shirt. He laid his arm on the end of the table. As Grandma undid each strip of towelling, Breda, Liam and I watched, our breathing soft and shallow.

At each turn of Grandma's arm, something fell out of the bandage and onto the table: tiny twigs, berries, coarse hair, and small bones. From the centre of the large wound on his arm, protruded a complete set of cat's teeth and held between them a sharpened stone. Grandma pulled at the teeth and stone with her bare hands until out they popped. Tumbling after them came dark, bloody entrails, feathers and apple green pus. But Granddad was saved.

If, on your travels around this world, you should see small, fenced-off areas of land thick with trees, which is never ploughed or dug from one decade to the next: leave them be.

The Instrument Bar

LATE SATURDAY MORNING AND I'M IN THE INSTRUMENT BAR, again. The Kawasaki Brothers are serving, doling out wit and sharp comments to all and sundry but being protective of the more fragile of their regulars, me included. A couple of bouncers from the Stage Door Club were in last night, spraying menace from the corner of the bar. I was up for a pint of Crooked House ale and I heard one say to the other,

'This place gets more like a mental hospital every f...ing day.'

They were referring to those of us who find solace in the bar while, for one reason or another, without regular employment. I was happy to ignore the comments but Kawasaki Jack was less tolerant. He leaned further towards them and lowered his voice an octave.

'You know he bit the nose off one guy while twisting his mate's balls so tight he was almost castrated,' he said.

Then he left their pints on the counter and walked down the far end of the bar to serve Molly Herring with a tonic water. He winked at me as he passed and shoved a pint glass beneath the Crooked House pump to show I was next in line. What he said was lies but it shut those guys up nicely.

Today the bar is up-a-height-busy with football

Saturday and a home game. The Kawasaki Brothers are full pelt keeping up with the drinks orders. Later, I'll be washing up and dodging round the chef, Boris from Budapest, who by late afternoon will be vodka'd-out and shipped home in Molly Herring's Volkswagen Camper for half the price of a taxi.

I'm anticipating an eventful afternoon. My gas fire blew up this morning and on the way here the cash point ate my credit card. Disasters always come in threes; it's an undisputed fact of my life.

'Hey Lou!' Kawasaki Dan shouts. 'Boris is in the Gents and needs loo paper, okay?'

At the same time as pulling two pints of lager he throws me the keys to get the toilet rolls. I bob round the side of the bar and when I open the supply cupboard, temptation smacks me in the teeth. There's a roll of twenty pound notes in a glass on the middle shelf next to the bleach. Probably put there for easy access after the first hour of the football rush; for security reasons the safe requires three staff members to be present in order to open it.

I stare at the money until Boris starts bellowing from the Gents, behind me. It's not a pleasant sound, a cross between a sow in heat and a cat being strangled. Without further internal debate I grab the money and stick it in my inside pocket. Then I take a six-pack of toilet rolls, shut and lock the cupboard door, hold my nose, take them into the toilets and throw the whole pack over the wall into Boris's pungent cubicle.

After he rumbles out like a bad tempered rhino, I nip in with the air freshener and make sure both cubicles are well stocked. Then I stand with my head resting on the cool tiled wall trying to convince myself to put the money back before it's too late. But the rent's due and the landlord's threatened to throw me out. A good bet on the nags would sort me out and if I catch an early race maybe nobody will know.

As I hand the keys back to Kawasaki Dan, he

holds my eyes a beat longer than necessary, checking me out. My spine frosts over. He puts the keys in his waistcoat pocket. When you've been repeatedly shat on as a child, trust is hard to come by, but for the first time in my life I've found it in this bar. So what am I doing?

Soon the United fans will head for the ground. It's a Premier League match today and they're up against Chelsea. The doors will be locked when they stream past later, either euphoric or mean as frustrated bulls. After a major defeat last year, they smashed the place up, leaving the Kawasaki brothers with broken limbs. But on the way to the match there's easy money to be made.

The roll of twenty pound notes is scorching my pocket. I glance round the bar. Molly Herring's a few feet away reading the Obituaries in one of the broadsheets. Seventy-five years old, white hair down to her bum, vintage dresses worn over tracksuit bottoms and hiking boots. She parks her camper van in the pub car park and lives there half the week. Nobody knows where she goes the rest of the time. She looks at me over the newspaper and slowly shakes her head. I tell myself she can't possibly know what I've done, until she takes out a powder compact and pats her nose with the puff. In the compact's mirror she has a fine view of the supply cupboard.

I walk over and sit beside her on a bar stool. She's part of my pub betting syndicate.

'Picked your horse?' I ask casually.

She says nothing for almost a minute. It's a long minute.

'Think again, Lou,' she says at last. Her lilac eyes drill into mine. I try to play it casual by shaking my head and shrugging.

'Your choice,' she says.

The odds are different now. Molly knows, but will she tell and if so, when? If I'm keeping the money I should skedaddle right away, but the thought of it creeps me out.

'Make the right choice, Lou,' Molly says as she goes over to join her friend, Stan, at his favourite table.

What's all this about choice? When did I ever get a choice? Mam took off and left us when I was six and I've been a betting machine since I was nine years old and sent to the Bookies every day by my old man. Even after he got struck off as a doctor for being drunk on the job one too many times, he'd steal money from Gran to feed his habit.

Don't sneer if you don't know the truth of it. It creeps up on you. The adrenalin, the elation, the awful addiction and then friends who lend you money and stop speaking when you don't pay them back and the bailiffs hammering at the door. I've been inside three times for thieving in order to bet. It's got worse with the internet. They've made it so easy, so anonymous and so glamorous. But this syndicate here at the bar, they trust me with their hard-earned bets and that should mean something. But nobody's ever looked out for me except me and that's what I'm doing now. I'm thirty-five tomorrow and there'll be no birthday cards on my mantelpiece.

Jenny waves me over. 'Your turn to pick the third gee gee,' she says. 'We've got *Grand Statue* in the 1.30 at Cheltenham and *Limder Hill* in the 2.15 at York. Have a peek at the paper. Stan's earmarked several that are good on form in the 2.30 and 3 o 'clock but it's up to you.' She touches my arm as she heads back to the kitchen. It tingles for some time.

I walk over to Stan's table. Molly Herring pointedly gets up as I arrive. Stan's just given up smoking and he's downing ten cups of coffee a day. He's got number five on the go now and his eyebrows are jittery. I slide on to the seat next to him and put my hand on the table, palm up.

'I'm not doing palms till the footie loonies have gone, Kawasaki Brothers' orders,' he says.

I give him the once-over trying to suss if Molly's told him about the money. His eyes are soft and his face generous, as usual.

'Do us a favour Stan, have a quick neb before I choose the third horse. It's in all our interests.'

But as Stan does a reccy on both palms I know it's not the gee gees I'm worried about, it's the roll of notes, all twenties, that are singeing my pocket.

'You're at a crossroad,' Stan says. 'One way there's sudden wealth, the other there's no pot of gold, just the same old same old but...' he pauses, examining my face before letting go of my hands.

'What?' I insist. 'What?'

He shakes his head and I know from experience that he can't be persuaded. He shoves the paper across the table for me to check out. He's marked up *Bling Bling* in the 2.30 at Cheltenham and *Emerald Eyes* in the 3.00 at York. They do nothing for my pulse and he's watching me too closely.

I pick *Magpie* in the 2.30 at Cheltenham, a thirty pound round robin on that, *Grand Statue* and *Limder Hill*. That's me, a magpie: an unrepentant thief attracted by glitter. I'm due at the bookies in half an hour and I've got the roll of notes – at least three hundred pounds – and the syndicate's thirty. I can see through the bar into the kitchen where the small television is on without sound, ready for the start of the race action at one.

I finger the notes in my pocket, prompting a spurt of adrenalin. Taking a deep breath I stand up and collect my jacket from the hat stand next to the supply cupboard. When I walk back past the bar, the eyes of all my betting syndicate follow me across the room, willing me to place a winning bet...or something else? I can't see the Kawasaki Brothers because the punters waiting to be served are six deep.

As I step out of the rotating door I almost flatten Lily, Molly's on and off partner. She's carrying a large cardboard box, probably more homemade steak pies for the lunchtime rush.

'All right Lily?' I say.

She shakes her head.

'I've been talking to Molly on the mobile.'

'Oh aye.'

'She told me, Lou.'

'About what?'

She nods her head slowly and sighs. 'Your choice,' she says as she steps around me and into the bar.

Out on the street everyone appears to be watching me. I stumble on the pavement a few times almost causing a domino effect among the busy shoppers. Is my body trying to make me stop and think again? Is it for once on my side? I suddenly trip and stagger. I've caught my foot in one of the postmen's plastic bundle ties and almost hit the deck but an arm reaches out and catches me.

I wish the owner of the arm had just let me fall. I deserve to be hurt. Sweat breaks out on my top lip as I remember, for the first time, the genesis of those words in my life. It was what Uncle Ray said as he battered the innocence out of me.

'Are you all right?' a voice says close to my ringing ears.

It's the woman who stopped me falling. She puts her hand on my shoulder and stares into my face.

'You look awful,' she says. 'Come on, my flat's just round this corner. I'll make you some sweet tea. It's supposed to help.'

'I don't deserve it,' I mumble, but she hasn't heard me. She's guiding me forward and she's surprisingly strong.

In her buttercup-painted kitchen I sit and sip the tea. My head is in total disorder.

'Do you often bring strangers into your flat?' I ask.

'Strangers?' she says, 'you're not a stranger, I see you in the Instrument Bar every week.'

I've never noticed this lovely woman in the bar. I'm far too busy staring at the bottom of a pint glass telling myself I deserve to be alone, deserve to be miserable, deserve to lose my money on the nags, time and time again.

'Of course,' I say. 'I didn't recognise you. Thanks for helping me out. I'm Lou.'

'And I'm Suzanne,' she says, shaking my outstretched hand.

In the bookies, the next-morning-hangover-sweat-stale-tobacco-stench assaults me. Some of the kids placing bets look about thirteen. Betty's taking the money and she's acting pissed off like she's suffering severe toothache. I watch the horses on TV walking round the paddocks, letting my brain rev and rev until it finds the right gear. When I catch Betty sizing me up I place the round robin thirty pound bet.

It's what Betty's used to but if I start handing over more high voltage notes, the hairs on her neck will stand to attention and she'll be on the phone to the Kawasaki Brothers toot sweet. They're a phenomenon all round here: two young brothers who turned up one day, each riding a Kawasaki motorbike and got work in the Instrument Bar. Now, five years later, they virtually run the place. They've made it a haven for misfits like me, setting us to work to pay for our food and drink. They don't take any shit though. Rights bring responsibilities: that's their motto. So I'm digging my own grave. For reassurance I reach into my pocket and touch the money. The familiar buzz isn't there. I touch it again, nothing.

I start laughing and only stop when the two bouncers from the Stage Door Club slither in. They walk over and crowd me without uttering a word. I can't move unless I push one of them out of the way.

'Doesn't look that hard, close up,' says crew cut.

'Just a feckin' loony really,' adds big ears.

'Let's be fair though, give him a chance to prove himself eh?'

'No Kawasaki brothers to protect him now.'

'Oy!' Lorna shouts. 'Outside for the rough stuff.'

I start thinking I deserve some aggravation for taking the money. Same twisted logic again but let's not get into any more of my tragic life story and what motivates me.

'You heard the woman,' says crew cut.

He pulls my arm round my back into a painful lock and pushes me towards the door, which big ears helpfully holds open. As I stumble onto the pavement, my jacket swings open and the roll of twenties falls out. All three of us stare at it, until big ears picks it up and rolls it between his fingers.

'Now then,' he says menacingly. 'What's this?'

'Yeah,' adds crew cut, 'what you doing with real money?'

Now I understand what a proper adrenalin surge feels like. The top of my head almost blows off. If they take the money, I'm totalled.

'Speak up,' crew cut says as he presses his face next to mine.

'It belongs to the Kawasaki Brothers,' I say.

'And they've given it to you? I don't think so.'

'It's for a bet.'

They exchange doubtful looks.

'Yeah. We got a tip. Molly Herring's uncle's a trainer.'

Oh, how the lies flow freely. But the situation is a learning curve. I understand perfectly what I have to do: take the money back to the Instrument Bar and 'fess up. It's the only road to freedom.

Crew cut lets go of my collar and shoves me into his pal. It's the old pass the parcel routine. When they've finished pushing me around, they push me to my knees.

'Name of gee gee?' Big ears demands.

'Aw no, I can't tell yer that. I'll get knacked.'

'You'll get knacked if you don't,' crew cut adds.

I do some deep breathing; make them think I'm frightened but actually everything is suddenly crystal.

'Come on lads, giz a break. It'll blow the whole deal if you start punting money on the same horse.'

'There's plenty other nag shops around.'

'You promise you won't put money on at Betty's?'

'Aye,' crew cut says, and big ears nods like a mechanical toy. In their eyes the greed grows.

'Give me back the Kawasaki's money then,' I say.

Big ears grabs the back of my neck.

'Shut it,' he growls.

'Listen pal,' I say. 'If yer steal this you'll not just have the Kawasaki Brothers after yer; the whole pub's put up for this bet.'

They exchange looks and my heart boom-booms. Crew cut nods at big ears and he shoves the money at me, almost knocking me off my feet.

'Name of gee gee?' crew cut demands

'*Magpie*,' I say, 'two thirty at Cheltenham. But for Judas' sake don't bet it all in one bookies. Split up, move the money around.'

Big ears lurches towards me, his hands bunched into sausage fists.

'You've got yer tip,' I say. 'Get cracking round the bookies. It's almost one fer feck's sake.'

Crew cut pulls him off and leads him away. I hear him ask big ears how much he's got in the bank and can't stop a grin almost bisecting my stupid face. I pitch round and run all the way back to the pub.

The crowd has thinned out and when I rush through the rotating doors into the bar the Kawasaki Brothers look in my direction. Molly Herring exchanges a glance with Stan and Lily. I walk slowly forward, trying to savour my Wild West Saloon moment. Pulling the roll of twenties out of my pocket I place it on the counter.

'I'm sorry,' I say. 'I was tempted and I gave in...'

The silence is caustic.

'We trusted you,' Kawasaki Dan says, his eyes like stones. Kawasaki Jack leaps over the counter. I have to stop myself from running out of the pub. He comes towards me until we're eyeball to eyeball.

'If it wasn't your birthday, I'd flatten you,' he says.

'And I'd help him,' Kawasaki Dan shouts.

'But he brought it back,' Molly Herring shouts out, 'that's how the story ends.'

The Kawasaki Brothers look at one another and nod. Kawasaki Jack picks up the roll of notes. 'This was your first month's wages,' he says, putting it in his pocket.

'Now you'll do the first month as a trial,' says Kawasaki Dan.

'You're taking me on the payroll?'

'Part-time,' Kawasaki Jack says. 'Don't fuck up again.'

At that moment, in order to prevent anything sentimental happening, Boris pushes through the door from the kitchen carrying a huge birthday cake covered in glittery candles. Because he's two-sheets-to-the-vodka-wind, he trips and the cake falls on to the bar before rebounding into my face. As if that wasn't enough, *Magpie* wins the 2.30 at Cheltenham, coming home at five to one.

City of Dreams

JANE FIRST MET MICHAEL NEXT TO A TRAMPLED FLOWERBED IN
Star Bank Park. She found him kneeling on the path,
keening and rocking as he pushed dozens of uprooted
geraniums back into the chocolate earth with his bare
hands.

'What happened?' she asked.

He waved his hands towards the other side of the
park. 'Oh, kids...you know.'

'Shall I help you?' She lowered herself to her
haunches.

He looked at her, his mouth slightly open. 'Thank
you,' he said, continuing to stare. 'But you'll ruin those
amethyst nails if you do. Perhaps you'd sing to me
instead?'

He looked about thirty but sounded older and his
face was sculpted with experience and humour. Jane
laughed with delight as he helped her to her feet and led
her to a nearby bench. As she sang from her eclectic
repertoire, he hummed along and carefully returned the
turbulent roots to the soil. When he'd finished he wiped
his hands on tissues, pulled her to her feet and danced
her along the path towards the park gates.

'Come and have a cup of tea,' he said as they hit
the street.

'OK,' she said, made bold by his playful attitude.

She thought he had a café in mind. Instead, he linked arms and led her to a row of Georgian terraces tucked away behind the park. Some were very grand with theatrical curtains and voluptuous objects in the windows and others, like Michael's, were divided into flats, many in need of affection.

'I...I don't know about this,' Jane said. 'I don't... well, we don't know one another.'

'I know you're kind and generous. You stopped to commiserate and you sang for me.'

'A café maybe?' she suggested.

'Fine but you'll have to pay, I haven't got any money with me.'

'My pleasure.'

In *Don's Diner*, where they were the only customers, they ordered sandwiches and a pot of tea.

'So Jane,' Michael asked between bites of tuna salad, 'how many times have you been in love?'

She stopped eating and stared at him.

'You're very....'

'Saucy?'

'No...'

'Bold?'

'Well...yes.'

He grinned and placed his hand on top of hers. She gently removed it.

'All right, how about your work, will you tell me about that?' he asked.

'I design fabric for curtains, wallpaper, bed linen and clothes.'

'How wonderful. Do you draw first, with a stubby B pencil, or go straight to brushes and paint?'

'I like to draw with a soft pencil...but it's all done on computers now so I have to fit in.'

He stared at her for a moment before speaking.

'You don't have to fit in, Jane. Nobody will give me a job because I don't fit in but I don't care.'

'But if you don't work, what do you live on and

how do you pay the rent?' she asked.

He did a windmill with his arms and although he smiled, his eyes were melancholic.

'My family has lots of money. The house I live in belongs to them and they let me have the rent from the other flats...as long as I stay away from their house.'

'That sounds cruel.'

'Oh yes, they're definitely cruel...' He paused, glancing at her under his eyelashes. 'But let's not talk about them.'

Not sure what to say, Jane focussed on her food but his eyes lingered on her face, making her skin hot.

'I like you Jane,' Michael said as he finished eating. 'You're bright and breezy and warm and...cuddly. If you like me too, I think we should buy a bottle of water and take it to the park for the disturbed plants. Then we should sit on a bench and do some kissing. How does that sound?'

'I think we should get to know each other a bit more before we think of...of kissing.'

He stood up and squatted by her chair, resting one hand very lightly on her knee.

'Jane, when I say kissing I do mean kissing, it's not some euphemism for sex.'

She examined his face and saw no guile. He leaned closer, resting his lips on hers. The movement was so gentle it could have been the wings of a dragonfly. He stayed in the same position for almost ten seconds before pulling away.

'See, that wasn't too bad, was it?'

'No, it was lovely.'

'Shall we do more or shall we head for the park?'

'A little more,' Jane said. This time she moved towards him and slightly parted her lips. Five minutes later the café owner pointedly began to cough. They stopped kissing and smiled at one another.

'Park then?' he said, getting to his feet.

Ignoring the café owner's raised eyebrows, Jane

paid the bill and bought a bottle of water. They walked along hand in hand. Michael sang some made-up opera to entertain her but before they reached the park she stopped and turned to him.

'I'd like to see your flat now,' she said. Being a designer she was convinced that the style a person lived in told you a lot about their inner life. She was also entranced by his kisses.

'Fine,' he said, turning round and gently pulling her with him. 'I like spontaneous.'

The hallway of the house was awash with discarded mail, flyers from hopeful tradespeople, coupons for washing powder and offers on pickled onions. When Michael told her he lived on the top floor, Jane sighed. She was a large woman and even the baroque banisters couldn't lessen the worry of climbing stairs that stretched upwards like the Tower of Babel.

Michael understood at once and peeled off his long scarf. He gave Jane one end to hold then wrapped the other around his chest before handing it over.

'I'm your animal of choice,' he said. 'Horse, donkey, bear, gorilla, lion or anything you want. I'll pull you up the stairs with accompanying sound effects. Right?'

'Right,' Jane answered with a surprised smile. 'A horse, now gee-up.'

Michael snorted and neighed his way up three flights, only pausing on the scanty top landing outside his flat door. Once there, he threw his scarf off and dropped down on all fours. 'Have I been a good horse?' he asked.

'Good boy, very good boy,' Jane said, stroking his hair in the spirit of the moment. Michael put his arms around her and squeezed the back of her thighs.

Jane was startled. She pushed him away and although unfamiliar words clamoured at the back of her teeth, she couldn't speak.

'Your thighs are wonderful, like pillows.' He got to his feet. His smile was artless so she said nothing.

After opening three mortise locks, Michael pushed back the door to his flat. Putting the slightest of pressure on Jane's lower back he ushered her inside. She had to turn sideways in order to get between the columns of newspapers on either side of the hall. They reached up to the ceiling.

'Takes me ages to read them all properly,' he said as he guided her into the kitchen. The walls were painted scarlet and the ceiling emerald green. He noticed her staring. 'It's good for hiding any splashes of blood,' he said. 'I'm always chopping bits out of my hands. Have a look round, I don't mind.'

The lounge was massive but every item of furniture, apart from one armchair was piled high with books and magazines. She walked slowly around the room and stopped by a large resplendent parrot in a cage the size of her bathroom. As she moved closer, it sidled along a wooden bar, observing her carefully with one pot-bellied eye.

'Woman on board...watch the language,' it squawked.

Jane laughed.

'I see you've met Pru,' Michael said as he walked in. 'Don't put your finger in her cage because she bites.' He stopped a few feet away. 'I'm sorry if I was a bit cheeky earlier,' he said, 'it's just that you smell so enticing and sometimes I forget myself. Do you forgive me?'

'If you promise not to do anything like that again.'

He looked baffled. 'What, never?' he asked.

'Never on a Sunday,' the parrot said.

'Shut up Pru. It's Wednesday and me and Jane are becoming acquainted.'

'How does Pru know I'm a woman?' she asked.

He laughed like a peal of rusty bells. 'She can smell you, just like a dog or a cat or I can.' Sniffing excessively, he moved towards her. She put her hand up to prevent him getting too close and he slowly sniffed each finger. 'Mmmmm, definitely a woman,' he said.

'And your scent is so seductive.' He snapped his teeth and Jane let out a small cry. He semaphored his arms like a string puppet. 'Carry on looking. I'm always curious about other people's places. I can't wait to see yours,' he said over his shoulder.

Jane's neck prickled at the thought of Michael in her small flat. She'd never met anyone so unsettled. His limbs and his mouth often seemed to work at odds with each other. It was strangely endearing.

There were three bedrooms, two mainly used for storage and the third, empty apart from the king size bed. Everything in it was inky blue: walls, carpet, curtains, bedclothes and the ceiling, which was covered in luminous stars.

Jane opened the wall cupboard, expecting to see clothes but there was only a large wicker laundry basket. Just as she was about to close the door she noticed a decorative strap hanging out of it. She lifted the lid. On top of some towels there was a woman's handbag. She pulled it out and wondered if it belonged to a girlfriend but there was no other sign of female presence. Hearing Michael's footsteps crossing the landing, she dropped the bag and the lid and closed the cupboard door.

'Do you think the room's too bare?' he asked.

'No, it's restful.'

'Good.'

She followed him back to the lounge.

'Hey ho hey ho, it's off to work we go,' squawked Pru.

'Just ignore her, she gets jealous of other females.'

'Really?'

'You do when you love someone...don't you?' He pointed to a chair he'd cleared for her.

Jane decided not to answer that question, instead she had one for him. 'Why don't your parents like you, Michael?'

'Oh, lots of reasons. They sent me off to boarding

school when I was six and I hated it. When I came home for my first weekend leave...' he paused. 'I'm sorry I haven't spoken about this for a long time. You have a way with you that encourages...intimacy.'

Jane shivered but said nothing.

'Anyway, I came home that weekend and at tea I blurted out what had happened to me...' He stopped again.

'You don't have to tell me if you don't want to,' she offered.

He pulled a red handkerchief out of his pocket and blew his nose. 'I said, *Dad, one of the Masters forced his prick into my bottom. The older boys called it buggery. I don't like it dad and it made me bleed, so please don't send me back there.*'

Jane gasped.

'My mother gasped just like that but dad put his hand firmly on her arm and without even looking up from his newspaper, said to me: *it will make a man of you and you'll soon get used to it.* Then he got on with eating his tea.'

'But that's terrible,' Jane said. 'He should have reported the teacher and certainly not sent you back there.'

'But he didn't report him and he did send me back and now he can't even bear to look at me because he says I'm a failure in life.'

'Michael, that's so unfair. I'm really sorry,' Jane said, although it seemed inadequate.

Later, when they got to the park with the water, police cars surrounded the area and the entrance was cordoned off. A very upright constable stood in front of the gates with his arms behind his back.

Beside Jane, Michael stopped abruptly. His body stiffened and he let go of her hand.

'What's happening?' Jane asked the constable.

'A woman was attacked here last night. Do you

live in the area?'

Before she could reply Michael said, 'No,' and catching hold of her hand again he pulled her away. When they were out of earshot he paused and looked into her eyes, saying, 'The police frighten me. They don't like people who are different.'

'Sometimes people upset me when they stare because I'm fat,' Jane said.

'Do they? But you're lovely, so soft, so sweet. I'd like to lick you all over.'

Jane pulled her hand out of his. 'I have to go,' she said.

'Are you sure?'

'I'm due back at work,' she lied.

He pulled a piece of cardboard out of his pocket and quickly wrote down his phone number. 'There,' he said, handing it to her. 'Phone me, please.'

Jane slowly walked away. She wanted to turn back to see if he was still standing there, but she didn't.

*

Two weeks after Jane met Michael, she couldn't stop thinking about him. She thought about him crying over the flowers and about his gentle kisses.

'He's a bit damaged and he's so unpredictable. It's a bit scary,' she told her friend, Debbie. They were having coffee and a sandwich before going to the cinema.

'What are you looking for Jane, someone so boring you can predict every move they'll make?'

'He did lie to the police.'

'That's not a hanging offence. He's probably got a problem with authority figures. Just answer me one question,' Jane said, pausing with a sandwich half way to her mouth.

'What's that?'

'Did he make you feel good?'

'Mostly, yes.'

'Not like that last toad you went out with who said he couldn't stand seeing you naked. Am I right?'

'Yes.'

'Of course he might have mental health problems but that's not a crime, is it?'

Jane spent two more days thinking things through before she eventually phoned Michael.

'Oh Jane, you rang, how totally brilliant,' he said. 'Will you come round? Shall I cook? Or should we meet somewhere?'

'I'd love to come for something to eat after work, say Friday?'

'Marvellous, what time?'

'Seven?'

'Spaghetti Bolognese all right?'

'Lovely.'

After she put the phone down she was exhilarated by the energy and enthusiasm in his voice. She rang Debbie.

'That's great, I hope you have a fab time, but make sure you get a taxi there and back... if you're coming back.'

Jane laughed. 'It's only a short walk to the Metro.'

'Another woman was attacked round there last night. They've got an identikit picture on the news of a guy they're asking to come forward.'

Feeling slightly uneasy, Jane rang off and switched on the TV. She'd missed the news but they trailed *Crime Watch* where they would later be doing a reconstruction. She cooked some rice and haddock, thought about Michael and then watched the programme with her dinner.

The presenter gave the dates and times of the attacks before switching to the reconstruction of a fair-haired woman walking through the park. The guy came from behind her out of some bushes, close by the flowerbeds where she'd first met Michael. Jane's scalp shrank a little. The man put his arm around the woman's neck and pulled her to the ground. He was dressed in

dark clothes with a Beanie pulled low on his forehead.
They gave out the phone numbers to call with any
information and then did a close up of the identikit
picture. Only the eyes had any real definition and they
were dark with strongly defined eyebrows. Jane
remembered that Michael's eyes were turquoise and she
let out a huge breath she didn't know she'd been holding.

On Friday she couldn't get out of work fast
enough. She rushed home to shower and change. On her
way back to the Metro she bought an expensive red wine
to go with the meal.

Apart from the top floor, Michael's house was in
darkness. She rang the doorbell and was greeted by Pru
squawking, 'What's the password? Come on, the
password?' Then Michael's amused voice saying, 'Sorry
Jane, she's being a real madam tonight. I'll put her back
in her cage and come down with my scarf. Hang on.'

Jane watched the lights coming on as Michael
came down each landing. When he pulled the front door
open she was jolted. He was wearing a papier-mâché
mask of a lion's head. He pulled it on top of his head to
speak. 'Thought we'd try a lion chariot this time, ok?'

He ushered her into the hall, took the proffered
bottle of wine, wrapped the scarf harness around his body
and began roaring as he took the stairs two at a time.
Jane was exhausted when they reached the landing and
had to lean on the wall to catch her breath. Michael pulled
a silk scarf out of his pocket.

'Do you mind if I blindfold you?' he asked.

Jane was dubious.

'Why?'

'It's a surprise.'

She breathed deeply as he put the scarf around
her eyes and as he led her down the hallway Pru started
squawking, 'You takes your chances, your money or your
life.'

If Michael hadn't been behind her she would have
run back to the door and away. When he slid the scarf off

she sighed, the lounge had been totally transformed. The furniture was clear of books and papers. The table was set with a white cloth, silver place settings, sparkling glasses and place mats with images of parrots. In a large candelabra three deep blue candles flickered in the breeze from the door.

'Oh Michael, it looks wonderful,' she said and she reached up to kiss him. He held her tightly, his lips soft on hers until Pru squawked,

'None of that hanky panky in here.'

Michael held Jane at arm's length, drinking her all in. 'I once worked in a zoo,' he said, 'that's where Pru came from, she was surplus to requirements and that's where she picked up some of her dodgy phrases.'

He took Jane's coat and sat her at the table. He already had a carafe of red wine open and he poured her a glass.

'Mmm that's delicious,' she said. 'Sort of plummy.'

'Yes it is.'

'Aren't you having any?'

'It doesn't suit me,' he said quietly.

'Oh?'

He moved from foot to foot, like a cat pummelling a cushion. 'Actually...it doesn't mix with my medication. Oh damn, now you'll be worried and think I'm crazy or a depressive and you won't come again...'

His sucked his bottom lip. 'But you're not someone who makes quick judgments like that are you? You've given me a second chance. And wait until you've tasted my Spag Bol; it's the best in the Western World.' He headed for the kitchen, doing a skip and a jump on the way. Then he shouted, 'Have a look at the new addition in the bedroom.'

The new addition was a large mirror on the wall facing the bed. A few seconds later, Michael came up behind her and rested his chin on her shoulder.

'You'll look so beautiful reflected in this in all

your glory,' he said.

Jane knew he was talking about her being naked and a small tremor hit the base of her spine. She wasn't sure if it was caused by anxiety or anticipation.

The spaghetti was excellent and there was a mixed salad with avocado and dressing. Pru's cage was covered, keeping her mostly silent. While they ate, Jane drank several glasses of wine and told him a potted history of her life. He was a good listener, which was another pleasant surprise. As Michael went into the kitchen to make coffee she checked her watch and was shocked to discover it was ten-thirty. If she intended to go home she had to leave soon or get stuck with the rowdies on the last Metro.

She paid a visit to the toilet. When she came out she could hear Michael clattering about in the kitchen and nipped into the bedroom to check the laundry basket. She didn't want to ask him outright about another girlfriend but she was curious to see if the handbag was still there. This time she found two handbags: the original and another, slightly larger one. Either he'd been seeing another woman since her previous visit or he had a fetish about handbags.

After coffee, Michael said, 'Listen Jane, I can tell you're a bit uneasy about staying the night so I have a suggestion. Either I'll walk with you to the Metro and then take you right to your door, or you can have the bed to yourself and I'll sleep in here on the sofa. And I promise you I will never try to get you into bed with me unless you really want me to. I know what it's like to be forced to have sex and I wouldn't wish that on anyone.'

He pulled the cover off Pru's cage. 'About bloody time,' Pru squawked.

'Tell you what,' Michael said. 'I always take Pru down into the garden about this time. She likes to have a fly about. Why don't you choose some music and relax?'

Jane stood up and put her arms around him. He responded with kisses on her neck and shoulders. She pulled his lips to her mouth and they kissed fiercely.

'I want to break free,' Pru squawked in a parody of the Queen song.

Jane and Michael laughed and fell on to the sofa. She pulled off his tee shirt and he unbuttoned her blouse. He sighed with delight when he saw her perfect plump breasts and buried his face in her cleavage.

'You're so self-satisfied I don't ne...ee...ed you,' Pru squawked.

'Shall we go into the bedroom?' Michael said. 'She'll shut up then.'

Jane nodded and once in the room with the door shut, she gave herself up entirely to the experience. At times she led Michael where she wanted to go and at other times she followed his desires. She could tell he wasn't judging her in the way some men had, comparing her to other sexual encounters or finding her body wanting and he wasn't wrapped up in his own technique. It was a genuinely mutual encounter and she enjoyed seeing her own body in the mirror, ripe and full and curvy against his lean, angular physique.

When they were done she snuggled into him, pulling the bedcovers around them but he was soon up on one elbow, brushing the hair off her face. 'If I don't take her into the garden for a while, Pru will wake us at five in the morning. I won't be long.'

Jane kissed his chest before letting him go.

*

The sun streamed through the window, shining onto the mirror and creating a light pattern on Jane's face. She sat up in bed. It took her a few seconds to remember what had happened the night before, including the second helping of sex sometime near dawn. When she was fully awake she heard singing. The sound was mournful and tragic. She climbed out of bed, pulling a sheet around her body and followed the sound. Michael was in the shower singing something vaguely operatic. He pulled her with him and kissed every inch of her body, until one thing led to another. Then, as she climbed out Jane noticed a large plaster on the back of his hand.

'Have you hurt yourself?' she asked.

'That was Pru, just an accident.'

'But you look sort of sad, is something wrong?'

'It was so beautiful, being with you... I'm just so happy.'

'So why do you look sad?'

'I always do when I'm happy. You'd better get used to it.'

'You nutter,' Jane said.

The change was dramatic and instant. Michael got to his feet, climbed out of the shower and brushed past her as he walked back into the bedroom.

'What's wrong?' Jane asked, following him.

'I don't like being called a nutter.'

'I didn't mean it like that Michael, it's just a figure of speech. Honestly.'

He had his back to her. She put her arms around him and rested her face between his damp shoulder blades. His heart thumped loudly against his ribcage. She waited for it to slow.

'I really am sorry Michael,' she said.

He turned and folded her into his arms. 'So am I. You didn't know that's how my family refer to me, and what kids at school called me.'

When he held her at arm's length she suddenly noticed that his eyes were brown, not blue. 'Your eyes...' she said.

'Haven't got my contact lenses in yet,' he said, with a smile. She pulled away from him and looked round, trying to see a clock. 'Are you still upset with me?' he said, picking up her tension.

'No...no, just checking the time.' She started pulling on her clothes.

'It's around ten. You don't have to go do you?'

She didn't but she wanted some space to think.

'I've arranged to meet a friend in the city.'

'Oh no...I've got croissants and eggs for breakfast. Can't you phone—'

'No, she's coming from York. I can't let her down. Sorry.'

With a bemused expression Michael watched her as she put on her shoes.

'You've gone all distant on me,' he said. 'Is it some kind of post-coital rejection?'

Jane paused. It had happened to her, men rushing to leave after a one-night stand. It didn't feel good. Her emotions were in uproar. She walked back to Michael and hugged him.

'She's a very good friend and I don't want to let her down.'

He nodded. From the other room Pru squawked,

'It's a sin to tell a lie.' Had the creature picked something up or was it just coincidence?

'I've got time for a quick breakfast,' Jane said.

Michael grinned and did a bow before heading for the kitchen. Some instinct made Jane check the wicker basket in the bedroom cupboard. There were now three handbags.

She crept out of the bedroom and along the hallway, quietly opened the flat door and ran down the three flights of stairs as quickly as she could. As she rushed towards Star Bank Park she heard, in the distance, Michael's voice calling her name. She didn't stop running until she reached a group of policemen standing in front of the park and then two of them had to hold her up to prevent her from collapsing.

'Excuse me,' she said. Her voice was raw and breathless.

They looked at her with disinterested expressions.

'The women who've been attacked,' she said. 'How many are there?'

'We're dealing with the third one now so if you would—'

Jane interrupted him. 'Did you find their handbags?' she asked.

At this, they all turned to face her, mouths open, like a group of mime artists.

*

The police had deliberately kept the information about the missing handbags from the media. Their way of weeding out lunatics who claimed to be the attacker. Jane was only half-awake through the statements, the questions and the identity parade. In the event, none of the attacked women picked out Michael. Two hadn't seen his face at all and the third one picked out a security guard who was delivering some forensic evidence to the station and had been roped in for the line-up. He did have dark hair and dark eyes.

But the handbags clinched it. They were all empty and although none of the contents were found in Michael's flat or elsewhere, his possession of them condemned him. His defence was that he'd found them in his garden. He claimed someone had thrown them over the hedge. But he had no alibi for any of the time frames when the attacks had taken place and his fingerprints were found on the outside of the bags.

During the trial Michael's face was haunted. When Jane gave evidence he looked away and as she left the witness box he closed his eyes and dropped his head. The jury took several days to reach a guilty verdict. He was sentenced to five years in prison for sexual assault with violence. The judge said he should serve the full term.

A month later, after weeks of sleepless nights and talks with Debbie, Jane went to the police. She was concerned about the lack of fingerprints on the handbags. If there was only Michael's on all of them and hers on one, she argued, then someone had wiped the bags clean.

'It doesn't make sense because women are always messing with their bags,' she said to the desk sergeant. He asked her to wait. Half an hour later a DCI Ross came and took her into an interview room.

'So...Ms Maloney...tell me about your concerns.

You were our main witness at the trial, so I'm interested in what you have to say.'

'Thank you for seeing me,' Jane said. 'I've been going over everything for weeks now. It's the handbags, their owners' fingerprints should be on them. I've never heard of a woman who doesn't constantly touch her handbag; tissues, purse, lipstick, metro pass, all of these things are in regular use. I think there's been an awful mistake.'

'But you were the one who turned him in, who came to us about the handbags in the first place.'

Jane sighed, took a tissue out of her bag and blew her nose. 'I was in a state of shock, I wasn't thinking straight.'

DCI Ross leaned back in his chair and rubbed his hands together. 'There were no other suspects, Ms Maloney.'

'But Michael wasn't picked out of the line up, was he?'

'Neither was anyone else.'

Jane sat forward and put her hands on the table. 'What about the security guard?'

DCI Ross snorted. 'You're clutching at straws now. The man was delivering a parcel to the station, he was a stranger, roped in to make the numbers up.'

'But he was picked out of the line up and he did have dark hair and eyes. Did you follow him up?'

DCI Ross opened the buff folder he'd brought into the room and leafed through its contents. Jane sat still and silent, though her breathing was shallow, like a startled cat.

DCI Ross closed the folder and slowly shook his head. 'It's too much of a coincidence. Imagine the odds against it...one, that he'd be delivering a parcel just as we were organising a line up and two, that someone would ask him to participate. Surely you can see that.'

Jane didn't answer straight away, she waited to see if Ross had anything else to say. When he didn't she blew out her breath loudly.

'Please say you'll follow him up. Just one unannounced visit to his house, that's all I'm asking.'

DCI Ross wouldn't meet her eyes. 'It would be a waste of police time. Now I'm sorry...but I think you're suffering from some sort of witness guilt —'

'I'm not suffering from anything inspector but I feel instinctively that I was wrong about Michael; I made a common mistake...'

DCI Ross raised his eyebrows. 'Which was?'

'That someone with mental health issues is more likely to commit a crime.'

'I can't reopen an investigation because someone has an instinct —'

Jane interrupted him by abruptly pushing back her chair and standing. 'Then I'll go to the media, DCI Ross. Miscarriages of justice are popular fodder, especially with the red tops.'

After a few seconds, he sighed loudly and stood up. 'Give me twenty four hours?'

'Yes, I will.'

The next day, DCI Ross rang Jane at work.

'You were right Ms Maloney. At the security guard's flat, we found items belonging to all of the women who'd been attacked. I owe you an apology. He'd been turned down to join the police force and he wanted to prove he was cleverer than us.'

In her flat that evening, Jane poured herself a large glass of red wine and planned what she'd say to Michael after he'd been released. And Pru, who she'd rescued from the RSPCA the day after the trial ended, nodded sagely as she listened to Jane's voice. However, it didn't prevent her from having the last word.

We live in the city of dreams...we ride on that highway of fire, sang Pru.

Once Were Angels Here

JAKE CORBETT LIVED ON A LARGE COUNCIL ESTATE IN NORTH East England. Sometimes, wandering about at night, he pretended he was an undercover cop making mental notes about the area and its inhabitants. Occasionally he whispered into an imaginary microphone taped to his shoulder:

> *- Two underage girls smoking tabs and swigging wine round the corner from the late shop.*
> *- A wrinkly shuffling off to the club to spend his pension.*
> *- Five lads on bikes patrolling the Metro station looking for targets.*

Nobody accidentally walked on to Jake's estate. It had invisible hazard signs at every entrance and word of mouth had made its reputation worse than reality. It was on the edge of Percy Main; close enough to the river not to be suffocating and only seven stops to the city centre on the Metro. Formerly a feeder estate for Smith's Ship Repair Yards, Swan Hunter's shipyards and heavy industry in Newcastle, it was now an everyone-for-themselves-type of place. The sense of community shared by those working in the same industry had been shattered by its decline. Many of the crackers who hung around the younger women on Jake's estate had never had a proper job, let alone any aspiration to have one. Women like his mam helped each other out, sharing cans of beans, bread, milk, coffee and ciggies, lifelines to the drowning. Mind, ten minutes later they could be brawling on the pavement knocking six bells out of each other.

But Jake Corbett had hope. When he reached fifteen he did four paper rounds, before and after school every day, to save enough money for the deposit and payments on a guitar. Out in Newcastle with his friend, Danny he'd seen it in the music shop, Zounds, near Pudding Chare. It was a Martin guitar with intricate mahogany inlays, a built-in pickup and the scent of success. He wanted it. The guy in the shop agreed it was his, on credit, if he came up with a hundred pounds deposit. To raise the deposit took him three weeks of early rising and playing hide and seek with dozens of bad-tempered dogs. He kept two paper rounds on to pay off the rest.

Jake enjoyed the emptiness of the early mornings. The streets were untroubled, frost lacquered the flowers and grass and there were no raised voices or sounds of angry hands on flesh. He liked reading the newspaper headlines, mostly tabloids on his rounds, but it made him feel in touch with a larger world.

He and Danny wrote their own lyrics and music and when Jake handed over the money and picked up his guitar, Danny was with him, as excited as he was. They went straight to North Shields and played until their fingertips were raw. Danny's parents had full time jobs so there was plenty of space to rehearse at his place.

'You're getting there,' Danny said as they finished playing that day.

'Danny man, I love writing the stuff but I'll never play guitar like you.'

'It'll come. If we're doing Busker's Night at the Trojan Rooms, we've got to find a singer. I'm useless on the high notes.'

'There's some lasses in my class might have a go.'

'What about you?'

Jake shook his head. 'It's not my scene.'

'What does that mean?'

'I'm not a front man. I'll talk to the lasses.'

Jake walked home along the riverside. As he turned off the path and up the bank to the road he saw a figure watching him. It was a tall man wearing a dark suit and pushing a shopping trolley. For a second Jake thought he heard his name being whispered but when he looked again there was nobody there. Back on his estate he held his guitar tight to his chest and moved swiftly along the streets, thankful for the police car that was patrolling the area.

When he opened the front door he sighed loudly. The kitchen stank of stale beer and tobacco. In the front room his mam and dad were yelling loud enough to crack the windows. It was about money, like always.

'There's no damned bread in the house, man, and my credit rating's long gone. You've got to do something, I don't get paid again till next week,' his mam shouted.

Jake could picture the scene: his dad lying on the sofa with a couple of empty lager cans on the floor and a bulging ashtray balanced on his chest; his mam standing over him, blocking the telly, forcing him look at her.

'I lay out thirty quid a week every Thursday from my giro. Where's that gone, eh?' his dad shouted.

'You steal it from my purse every Friday.'

His dad had been a riveter at Swan Hunter's shipyard. When the yard closed he went to the dogs, literally. Spent every penny of his redundancy on the hounds, came back drunk, broke and miserable every time. He shattered Jake's mam's heart and her aspirations for a little bed and breakfast place in Whitley Bay, dishing up the best food for miles around, with satisfied customers returning year after year. Instead she worked as a school dinner lady during the day and pulled pints at the CIU club three evenings a week. His dad had been barred from the club after an untidy brawl with one of the committee men.

That night, with his new guitar warm in his hands, Jake chose to ignore his parents. And anyway, Brenda, who lived on the next street, had warned him,

'Yer mam's got to decide when she's had enough Jake, not you, otherwise when he comes slavering back with a bunch of daffodils in his hand and soft words on his tongue, she'll keep taking him back. Believe me I know what I'm saying.'

Once in his room upstairs, Jake left his door open. He needed to hear in case his mam called for help so he played soft acoustic, trying out the guitar in different tunings, and putting it through its paces. With his window open he could hear the usual melody of traffic, dogs barking, sirens, road works and pigeons murmuring on the roof but none of it drowned out the tuneless bellowing from downstairs.

Forty minutes later, with a slam of the back door, it finally stopped. Jake put the guitar to sleep in his small wardrobe, pulling his clothes around it so that it couldn't be seen. That night his dreams were uneasy. He kept jumping awake, expecting to see his dad leaning over the bed, fist raised.

He was up early and out on his paper rounds. He saw a girl from his class, Melanie Hart, pushing a wheelchair down towards the river. Catching up with her he nodded and glanced at the guy she was pushing. He was thin as a twig with wizened, leathery skin. A half-smoked ciggie drooped from his bottom lip.

'It's mi dad,' Melanie said. 'He's got cancer, from smoking and some process at the shipyards. He likes to sit and watch the river.' Jake raised his eyebrows. Girls were still a mystery to him. 'Mam buggered off last year with a bricky from Shields,' she continued.

'Bloody parents,' Jake muttered. 'Hey Mel,' he went on, 'Can you sing?'

'Wish I could.'

When Jake had finished his rounds he called at Bobz Burger Van and fuelled up with an egg sandwich and strong coffee. As he stood leaning on the back of the van, eating and staring out at the river, he saw the tall man again, this time pushing the shopping trolley along the bank. Again he stared at Jake and again there was that soft whispering in his ear. A blink later the man was gone. Jake put it down to lack of sleep.

At home later, his dad was missing and his mam looked shifty. Oven-cooked fries and a new bottle of tomato sauce decorated the table; it wasn't her style.

'You've had your hair done,' he said.

'Yeah, d'you like it?'

She couldn't meet his eye. Jake pushed his chair back and ran upstairs. His guitar was gone. His mam backed away as he ran into the kitchen.

'Where is it?' Jake shouted. 'What's he done with it?' When his mam flinched he blew out his breath in a long sigh. 'Just tell us where he's taken it.'

'He took it to Chancers. He's only pawned it till he gets his giro. You'll get it back.'

'He's gone to the dog track to lose it all, hasn't he?'

'Y'never know Jake, mebbes this time...' she tailed off, knowing as well as Jake that the big win would never come.

Jake ran up to his parent's bedroom and pulled a chair over to the wardrobe. There it was in a transparent suit bag, his dad's leather motorbike jacket with embroidered badges all over the back from his early days racing at the Isle of Man and elsewhere. Jake took hold of it and stepped down.

'No Jake,' his mam said. 'You can't take that. It's vintage, he'll go ballistic.'

'Tough fucking luck; he can get a job like me and buy it back.'

The guy in Chancers was reluctant to do the swap at first,

kept glancing at a group of lads barely out of primary school, who were harassing customers outside the *Late Shop* next door.

'Get us some cider,' they shouted. 'What about some tabs or a couple of cans?'

The pawn guy was worried they'd turn their attention to his shop. In the past some kids had set fire to his place; you could still see the charred wood. Jake used the guy's anxiety.

'Listen pal,' he said quietly. 'I've worked for that guitar and he had no right to bring it here. Give it to me in return for his jacket and you'll hear no more from me. Or...' Jake left the unspoken threat hanging.

'I'm closing up now,' the guy said, glancing outside.

Jake followed his gaze, 'Not until I've got my guitar back you're not.'

Back home, the air was shimmering with static. His mam's face was red and blotchy. His dad wasn't in sight and there was no telltale drone of the TV from the front room. Jake went into the hall and started up the stairs to chill in his bedroom. His dad was waiting for him on the landing, his sour whisky breath stealing oxygen from the atmosphere.

'Where's my fucking jacket?' he asked.

'Same place you took my fucking guitar.'

'You bastard.'

He rushed at Jake, nutting him on the bridge of his nose. Jake winced and fell forward. His dad ripped the guitar off his back, breaking the strap in the process.

His mam called his name.

'Go to Brenda's, mam. I'm fine,' Jake said.

His dad was holding the guitar out in front of his body. 'Go and get my fucking jacket, now!'

'No.'

'Yer can't even play the friggin' thing you useless chiseller.'

Jake stared at his dad and balled his hands into tight fists.

His dad brought the guitar crashing down on top of the banister. The crack of the wood was like an ice pick in Jake's neck. He stood still, numbed. Throwing the half broken guitar on the ground, his dad jumped and stamped on it until it was a dangling mess, then pointed at it.

'That'll be your fucking head if you come any closer. Now clear off and get my jacket,' he shouted.

Jake stared at his dad's bulging eyes, the froth at the corners of his mouth and his skin, crimson with rage. Downstairs, his mam opened the front door and left. Jake lunged forward and picked up the decapitated neck of the guitar. He aimed it at his dad's head but only got a swipe at his shoulder as his dad ran into the bathroom and locked the door.

'You'll never see that jacket again,' Jake shouted before heading downstairs.

At Brenda's, his mam was sobbing. 'She can stay the night here,' Brenda said.

Jake nodded and left, losing himself in the darkening streets. He kept going hot and cold. He was due at Danny's to rehearse but his guts had turned to concrete. Making his body tall, he pulled the hood of his sweatshirt forward, moving with a kicking stride and swaggering shoulders. It was getting towards dusk, and danger gathered in the shadows.

As Jake turned the last corner before leaving the estate, he came upon the extended Harrison family spread wide across the street and pavement and ripe for confrontation. Turning back or changing direction was not an option. He had to keep his line and plough straight through hoping nobody challenged him. If they did he had a hard-earned reputation of his own to defend.

No one spoke. Seconds later Jake knew why; the oldest Harrison son, Karl, was marching down the street towards him in a brand new army uniform. As he got level with Jake he slowed down and grinned.

'Time to give them A-rabs over in 'fganhistan some shit they won't forget,' he said, mimicking an American accent.

'They're not Arabs,' Jake said. Fortunately, Karl didn't wait for a response.

As Jake slipped away, his thoughts crashed about. No way was he becoming a Harrison clone: drawing benefits, smoking sixty tabs a day, drinking enough alcohol to provoke his liver into revolution, visiting the clap clinic on a regular basis and joining the army.

Once clear of the estate he pelted down to the river and paused on an old railway bridge to still his racing pulse. He loved the river Tyne; the secrets it carried, the muck from what little work still went on, the boats travelling from here to there. Huge ferries off to Amsterdam and Scandinavia, repaired military vessels, fishing boats and recently, more and more yachts.

He planned to walk along the makeshift footpath to the coast to tell Danny it was all over. No more daydreaming about music, he'd find some other way to escape, even if his only immediate options looked like drug dealing or thieving. As he turned to leave he heard an amazing voice, singing. It was opera or some such thing and it caught him in an arm lock.

It was coming from under the bridge. Quietly, he clambered down the scrub to the track, looking through the bushes to see who was there. It was the tall man he'd seen before, now standing on the riverbank, one hand on the shopping trolley. Under the bridge was a well-known haunt for dossers, which is what Jake assumed the man was.

As he listened, a second voice joined in. He stared but in the dim light he couldn't see anyone else. The performance became an incredible duet shimmying between the two voices, one mellow and bass, the other an unbelievably high trill. They were like magnificent birds with only him to appreciate their talent.

Leaning back on the grass Jake gulped in the sounds. As they finished singing, tears drizzled his cheeks. He quickly wiped them away. Leaning forward the man placed something like a large parcel in the shopping trolley and then turned briefly to look in Jake's direction before walking away from him and away from the coast.

Intrigued, Jake followed at a distance until the man met up with more winos. They'd made a large blanket on the tough grass with flattened cardboard boxes. From Jake's viewpoint it almost looked like a picnic. There was much laughter and swapping of bottles. As Jake crept closer he thought he was being watched, although the drinkers all had their backs to him. He wondered if people living rough developed an instinct for intruders.

The tall singer settled on the ground to roll a cigarette and accept a swig from bottle or two. Jake didn't want to be seen by the winos. Recently, a bit further along the river, some lads had attacked one of them and started a brawl. The lads came off worst, two of them stabbed, one in the leg and one in the arm but it hadn't cooled their animosity.

As Jake moved closer to the abandoned shopping trolley, his breathing became shallow. He squatted on the ground and stared through the wire lattice of the trolley, hoping for more singing. Out of the corner of his eye he detected a movement to his left, but before he could turn, something small and cold touched his face. Jake leapt to his feet, cursing.

The winos turned their wolf eyes in his direction, and one shouted,

'Everything all right?'

Jake was confused. Could they see him? Were they talking to him? All at once, a voice rose from inside the trolley; the sound was melted honey,

'No problemo,' it said.

Jake closed his eyes to accustom them to the dusky light and again lowered himself down on his haunches. When he re-opened them he was staring at a face from an infant school drawing lesson; one eye higher than the other, oversized nostrils and a large, full mouth with buck teeth resting on its lower lip.

'I'm Eddie-mi-lad,' the voice said. 'Who are you?'

'Jake…Jake Corbett,' he replied. His voice was unsteady. Eddie-mi-lad had no limbs, just a large head and a small torso resting on a velvet beanbag. Remaining crouched, Jake turned his head away. He had no idea what to say.

'Look at me,' Eddie-mi-lad said. Jake didn't respond. 'Look at me. The more you look the less strange I'll appear.'

Slowly Jake turned his head, until he was face to face with Eddie-mi-lad. He noticed his lavender eyes with their velvety lashes and his skin, as smooth and soft as duckling down. Eddie-mi-lad smiled. It didn't improve his looks but Jake felt ashamed of his earlier reaction.

'And what are you doing here, Jake Corbett?' A loud voice asked from behind him.

Jake turned and looked up at the milky face of the tall singer. In the shadows behind him, the rest of the winos were alert and watching.

'Nothing,' Jake said, jumping to his feet.

'Nothing, is it? Then why are you sneaking about? Why not walk out in the open if you're up to nothing?'

Jake made to leave but three winos blocked his path. Their eyes were steady and determined. The tall singer moved closer to Jake, put a hand on his shoulder and stared hard at him. Jake tried to shrug him off but he couldn't move. When the man straightened up and turned away, Jake shivered.

'He's all right boys,' the singer said. 'He has an interest in music.'

'How do you know that, have you been following me?'

'I think you'll find you've been following me, Jake. Oh, but we all like a sweet lyric or two, don't wehboys?' He said. The winos all vociferously agreed. Eddie-mi-lad laughed; it was the sound of glass chimes in the wind. 'Well Jake, if you give us one of your songs, we will oblige, in return. Agreed?' the singer said.

'I can't...my guitar is...isn't here.'

'Sing my boy, sing,' the man said before turning to the winos.

'I can't...I don't sing.'

'He needs backing, lads,' the singer said. 'Tonto, give me a lend of your fiddle, will you? And Eddie-mi-lad, there's a bit of harmony for you to join in on, right?'

'Your wish is my desire, Sibylline,' said Eddie-mi-lad.

Jake was open-mouthed as he watched an old, but pristine violin appear from among the horde of winos.

'Well?' The man said.

Jake worked through lyrics in his head, the man tuned the instrument and Eddie-mi-lad did a few breathtaking scales to warm up.

'Which key do you prefer my boy?' the man asked.

'I can't sing,' Jake said again.

'Oh but you can. What do you say Eddie-mi-lad?'

'If you think he can sing, Sibylline, then he can.'

The man stared at Jake and played a scale on the violin. 'You have raw talent Jake...use it. Follow me on the scale, do it inside your head.'

'I've told yer. I can't.'

'No such word in my world, Jake,' Eddie-mi-lad said.

Everyone stared at Jake, like they were willing him to sing.

'Believe me Jake, you can do it. Take a deep breath, right from the bottom of your belly.' The singer laid the bow on the violin strings and played.

After a few seconds Jake took a breath and sang

along. Once, twice, three times the man played the scale and each time Jake's voice improved.

'Pitch perfect,' Sibylline said as he stopped playing. 'It's a gift, isn't it lads?'

Eddie-mi-lad and the winos cheered. 'So, any preference now as to key?' Sibylline asked.

Jake shook his head.

'Right then, you just start singing and we'll pick it up. Do the chorus first. Feed your breath into the song, Jake. Breathe in at the start of each line.'

Jake felt slightly crazy. He was surrounded by a bizarre sort of chaos and a man who seemed to know too much. At the same time, excitement churned his stomach. Taking a deep breath he began to sing one of the songs he and Danny had written:

> *'And the sea will swallow our world*
> *turn concrete into pearls*
> *it will forget we ever lived here*
> *and turned paradise into a scar on the universe,*
> *scar on the universe is what we are.'*

By the time Jake reached the end of the first line of the chorus, the violin was in full swing, hitting each note and adding new ones with a mouth-watering precision that he and Danny had only dreamed of achieving. Eddie-mi-lad joined in halfway through the first line, taking the harmonies into orbit, fluting and warbling in unworldly ways. Everything was fluid, full of possibilities. As Jake reached the end of the last chorus, he laughed loudly, throwing his head back with pleasure.

The winos applauded with amazing gusto, coming forward to pat him on the back or shake his hand. As they turned away towards their makeshift campsite, feathers drifted out of their bulky overcoats; twenty or more of them, large feathers in every shade of yellow floated on the air and rose up towards the navy sky.

'Our turn to perform now lads,' said the tall singer. 'Wet the vocal chords and let's get at it. This lad has places to go.'

Jake was stuck to the earth. He pinched his skin; it wasn't a dream. He could sing. Sibylline cleared his throat, picked up Eddie-mi-lad and placed him in the crook of his arm. Tonto played an intricate opening melody on the violin and the singing began. This time it was Eddie-mi-lad who started and the man who brought new themes and harmonies, and all supported by an amazing chorus of winos. The words were in a language foreign to Jake, but it didn't matter.

Strangest of all, even though he could see Sibylline singing there in front of him, with Eddie-mi-lad on his arm, he could also hear him whispering in his ear,

'Music is salvation for us all.'

Jake closed his eyes and the sound carried him off. As it eventually faded, a dog licked his face. Its breath was fishy and acrid.

'What's up?' His friend Danny said, dropping his bicycle to the ground and leaning over him. 'What's happened to your face?'

Jake looked around. He was lying awkwardly at the bottom of the bank where he'd first clambered down from the road to the path. He jumped up, and ran along the riverside with Danny and his dog, Sid, following on behind.

The flattened cardboard was still on the grass. One or two bottles lay here and there and, lying on its side was the empty shopping trolley. He stood silently staring until Danny put a hand on his shoulder.

'You all right pal?' he asked. 'Has someone mugged you?'

'No...no, I'm fine.'

'Sid and me got worried when you didn't turn up. What's the score like?'

Jake shook his head, unsure what to say. 'What time is it?'

Danny checked his mobile, 'Nearly seven.'

An hour missing. It had been before six when he'd first heard the singing.

'So, you still coming to mine then?' Danny asked. 'I'll give you a ride on the pannier rack.'

'Aye, why not?'

On the way to Shields Jake told Danny about his dad and the smashed guitar.

'That's crap behaviour. You should report him, get it on record.'

'Waste of time.'

Once in Danny's basement Jake stopped trying to figure out what had happened to him on the riverbank. There was a stillness in him and fresh confidence.

'Play the new song,' he said to Danny.

'You can use my acoustic.'

'No,' Jake said. 'You play, I'll sing.'

Danny stared at him for a second before shrugging his shoulders. When Jake began singing, Danny nearly fell off his stool. His friend's voice was confident and strong.

'Hey man,' Danny said, putting the guitar down. 'That really was something and you said you couldn't sing.'

'Well, I can.'

'Yeah, but...'

Jake blew out a long breath. 'Some winos showed me how.'

'Yeah right.'

'I dreamt it.'

'Come on man, share.'

'You wouldn't believe me.'

At that moment, Danny's dad popped his head round the door. 'Fancy some lasagne?' he asked, holding out a tray with two bowls of pasta and some Parmesan cheese. Danny took the tray and they ate like starving men.

Danny's parents were always friendly and welcoming but Jake still felt uncomfortable with them. He was used to people who lived on the edge, who didn't have space in their heads for books and films and theatre.

Ten minutes later, he and Danny were getting ready for some more rehearsal when Danny's parents came into the basement. Jake looked at Danny, who pulled an embarrassed face. 'I said we'd play that new song for them because dad offered to ferry us to and from The Trojan Rooms when we do the gig there.'

Danny's parents sat on the old sofa, watching them, eyes glittering with anticipation. As Danny tuned up, Jake's confidence began ebbing away. He closed his eyes. He saw Eddie-mi-lad's face, grinning; he hadn't allowed his disadvantages to stop him singing. That thought dissolved Jake's fear. He took a deep breath and stood up.

Their performance was spot on. Danny rose magnificently to the challenge and his parents were thrilled.

Danny's dad drove Jake home, stopping, as usual on the main road. In his quiet way he made it clear to Jake that he and his wife, Claire, would support both him and Danny if they wanted to take their music seriously.

'There's this music scholarship I found out about and I think you'd be eligible. I'll get the details. OK?'

Jake couldn't find the right words to thank him, but before getting out of the car he shook his hand.

As he walked through the estate his head was full of Sibylline and Eddie-mi-lad but he had no computer access at home and anyway his dad was prowling around the garden with a bottle in his hand, looking for trouble. Jake went to Brenda's and stayed the night.

After school the next day he slipped into the IT suite and got Melanie Hart to lend him her password. She was curious and stayed.

'I want to find out about opera and a man called Sibylline and someone called Eddie-mi-lad,' he told her.

Melanie loaded the relevant words into the search engine and when the options came up, clicked on the first one. There, Jake discovered that Sibylline, real name Harry Fisher, was born on Tyneside. He read on:

'Harry Fisher was an outstanding operatic performer often compared to The Great Caruso and in constant demand all over the world. He travelled extensively performing works by all the great composers. It was an immense tragedy that in 1959, while he was in Italy, his pregnant wife, Marie, had trouble sleeping and the doctor prescribed a new drug, Thalidomide. The baby was born without any limbs. It wasn't the only damaged baby. It was a gigantic scandal.

Harry Fisher gave up touring and helped to raise the boy, who they nicknamed, Eddie-mi-lad, and he got his reward when it turned out that the child had the voice of an angel. As the boy grew they started successfully singing together. But Fisher's wife never fully recovered from the experience, and when the boy was ten years old she drowned herself in the River Tyne. The opera, 'Once Were Angels Here' is the story of this tragedy. It opens with the birth of the boy and ends with his wife's death.'

'And I know where she drowned,' said Jake, forgetting Melanie was standing behind him.

'Do you?' she asked, leaning forward. 'It doesn't say where, just the River Tyne. Oh, but look at the date she died...'

'Yes, I know, October twenty first, the same date as yesterday.'

'Yeah, but over thirty years past and see,' she pointed at the screen. 'The guy and his son only died a few years back.'

Jake turned to face her. 'Do you believe in Angels, Melanie?' he asked.

She nodded and touched his hand. Jake smiled. They walked back to the estate together. At Jake's gate, his dad stood waiting, his face contorted andmalevolent. Jake and Melanie turned away. Music had taken others out of hell, Jake told himself, and it would do the same for him.

An Immodest Proposal

'YES, IT'S A NICE PLACE BUT IT'S TOO FAR OUT,' JOHN INSISTED.

'The drive home will help you relax and wind down,' Louise said.

He snorted; usually a sign that he thought the argument was over. But she hadn't finished.

'You can leave your work behind, come back to your family, the lovely countryside and fresh air,' she went on.

John snorted again. 'But if I have things to do in the evenings I'll have to stay in the city all day and drive home in the dark.'

'You're at university doing a PhD, it's not like you're a surgeon, on call at all hours. A lot of the time you'll be able to work from home.'

'Oh, what, with a screaming baby in the next room?'

They'd been arguing since they left the farm. She'd loved the place. It was half a large, old farmhouse with only the bathroom to share with the farmer, his wife and two small kids. There was an orchard with plump pigs, cows in the fields and fantastic purple hills as a backcloth to the trees and pasture land.

Louise was relieved that she'd left baby Amy with her mother in Yorkshire. The journey would have been a nightmare for her. They were moving in five weeks, at the end of July, to give them time to settle in before John started his PhD research post. They had six more places to view, all flats and all of them in the city.

The roads were typical rural Devon, narrow with lofty hedges and poor visibility. Louise braced herself by grabbing the dashboard every time John took a blind corner too fast. She knew, from past experience, that if she commented he'd drive even faster so she chewed her lip and spawned knots in her neck.

'Will you at least consider the farm, not just dismiss it? When we've seen all the places we can have a bite to eat and talk it through,' she said.

John rowdily exhaled. 'You're wasting your time. You'll never convince me. I want to be in the city,' he said.

'Then why did you bother to go and see the farm?'

'It was on the way,' he said, taking his eyes off the road and giving her one of this jaded glances.

She clutched the sides of her seat.

'I think you should let it go now,' he said.

Louise sighed; she was out of sync with him and suspected he was deliberately driving too fast, as an aid to winning the argument and to show her how stupid it would be to live out in these backwoods.

'What about what I want?' Louise said, trying to keep her voice even. 'You're expecting me and Amy to leave family and friends and move hundreds of miles with you but I don't have any say in where we live?' When he didn't respond, she stared at the side of his head and saw his flexed jaw muscles. He accelerated again.

She turned her attention back to the road and up ahead, in a break in the hedge, she caught a glint of chrome. 'Slow down, please,' she asked.

They were approaching another blind corner. John didn't slow down. Louise saw the milk tanker before he did. It filled the narrow road. There was no space to pass. John braked and turned the car into the hedge. Just before they crashed Louise looked up at the tanker driver. He was driving with one hand and lighting a cigarette with the other. He hadn't even seen them.

Everything became muffled and blurred. The sound of the crash, John shouting, her realisation that she'd taken her arm out of the seat belt to wipe the windscreen a few seconds earlier and the sensation of flying.

The seatbelt partially held her body but the top of her head hit the windscreen hard enough to crack the glass. Louise felt nothing. Her efficient bio system put her out of action while it dealt with the crisis. When she surfaced – briefly – she was being carried on a stretcher. Her head was cushioned so that she couldn't move it. All around her blue lights flashed. She caught a quick glimpse of John as they loaded her stretcher backwards into the ambulance. He was talking to a police officer. He glanced at the ambulance then turned away. Another officer appeared beside her and took hold of her hand.

'You'll be fine,' he said in a soft, West Country brogue. 'I'll follow you to the hospital. My name's Alan.'

Her eyes closed at the same time as the ambulance doors. When they re-opened she was in an emergency day ward and PC Alan was sitting beside her bed reading a newspaper.

'Hello,' he said. 'How are you doing?'

'I've been better.'

'Of course you have. I'll fetch the nurse and she'll tell you what's happening. Don't go away.'

Louise smiled. He was the sweetest policeman she'd ever encountered.

He returned with a nurse who was hanging on his every word. It wasn't that he was classically good looking, he was too slim and his eyes were too pale for that. But there was a warmth and delicacy in the way he dealt with people and his smile was magnetic.

'Well Mrs Davies, you've had a close shave, so to speak,' the nurse said. 'But the scan we did shows no internal damage, so, one very lucky person.'

Until she let it out in a long sigh, Louise hadn't

realised she'd been holding her breath. 'What happens next? Can I leave? Is my husband waiting?'

Alan and the nurse exchanged a meaningful glance but Louise had no idea what the meaning of it was.

'Alan...PC Morley, is going to take you to a cottage hospital outside Exeter, on the Tiverton road. They'll keep you in overnight and make sure everything's fine before letting you out into the big bad world again. And you'll have a sack of painkillers to ease you through the night. All right?'

'If you say so,' Louise said. She'd received the unspoken message that John was not pacing about in the waiting room with lines of worry eating into his face.

The nurse pulled the curtains around the bed.

'Your clothes are a bit of a mess but we've parcelled them up for you and in the meantime the WRVS have produced these elegant items.'

She held up a tweed skirt that would have suited a retired teacher, a pale blue twin set, a slip, some tan tights and a bra that looked three sizes too big and must have been second world war surplus.

'Excellent. I can pretend I'm my own great-grandmother.'

Alan and the nurse laughed and took themselves off so that she could put the clothes on.

Once she was on her feet Louise checked the locker for her mobile. It was there but the screen was smashed and it wouldn't work. She dressed slowly. Her head was painful and if she moved it too fast she became dizzy. When she checked the rest of her body she found multiple bruising, cuts and all her nails had been badly broken. She wondered if John had been injured.

Alan was waiting at the end of the ward. He rushed over when he heard the curtains swish and insisted she took his arm.

'Where's my husband?' she asked.

Alan shook his head.

'Do you know when he's coming?'

'I'm afraid not.'

There was something in his eyes.

'The hospital will let him know were you are.'

Louise nodded.

'You don't look half bad you know,' Alan said. 'Your bone structure is perfect.'

Louise smiled. He was trying so hard to cheer her up,

'Do I detect a sculptor in policeman's clothing?' she asked.

'How clever of you. It's actually painting. I've been going to evening classes for two years.'

'Are you any good?'

'Ouch, you don't mince your words do you?'

'Sorry, I didn't mean to be so abrupt.'

'That's fine. I like it. Give me a straight talking woman any day.'

He helped her into the car as if she was made of porcelain. He drove steadily, keeping his attention on the road at all times. Louise felt safe. She told him why she and John were in Devon and about their argument and then immediately felt disloyal. She rested her head on the seat and fell asleep until he manoeuvred the car over road bumps at the entrance to the cottage hospital.

They had a ground floor room prepared for her. It looked out over lush woodland with purple hills in the distance. They were the same hills she'd seen from the farm garden. With a rush of emotion, she knew she wanted to gaze at them every day, to watch Amy growing up strong and healthy alongside dogs, hens, cows and the sweet scent of the apple orchard.

'This is lovely,' Louise said as she eased herself into one of two floral armchairs close to the window.

'Can I get you a drink or something to eat?' Alan asked. 'You've been out of action for hours, you must be hungry.'

'I'd rather you told me where my husband is,' she said.

He raised his eyebrows a few centimetres. 'He's arranging stuff to do with the car. I think he's had an insurance assessor out to the garage where it was towed and I believe they've said it's a write-off. Last I heard he was trying to organise a hire car. We're keeping him informed.'

Louise sensed disapproval in Alan's tone.

'Was he hurt?'

'A few minor cuts and bruised chest.'

'He'll be desperate about seeing the other flats,' she said.

'Probably.'

'We have to go back to Yorkshire tomorrow.'

Alan nodded. She didn't quite know why she was defending John but decided to change the subject anyway.

'You don't have to stay with me all the time,' she said. 'There's a bell to call a nurse. You must have loads to do.'

'I'll stay unless you really want me to leave you alone.'

'No, I didn't mean that. It's nice having you here. But there must be more urgent things for you to do.'

Before he could reply, there was a knock on the door and a nursing sister came in. She was around fifty, tall and curvy with sympathetic eyes and an Irish accent.

'Hello Mrs Davies, I'm Sister Donovan, Lottie. Hello Alan.'

He nodded. 'Nice to see you, Lottie.'

'We'd like you to get undressed and into bed Mrs Davies...'

'It's Louise.'

'Louise...it's just a precaution. If there was a sudden deterioration in your condition, having you in bed would make things easier for us and I think proper rest will help you recover. Alan can stretch his legs while I help you into one of our delightful hospital gowns.'

After she'd tucked her in, Sister Donovan took

her blood pressure and pulse. 'You seem to have made a big hit with Alan,' she said.

Louise frowned, not sure what she meant. The sister picked up her confusion.

'I'm assuming you were alone in the car and that's why Alan suggested transferring you here.'

'He did?'

'Yes. It's his afternoon off and he said he would keep an eye on you.'

There was something in her expression that Louise couldn't fathom.

As Lottie left, Alan returned with a pile of newspapers and magazines. He put them on the bedside table. 'I fancy a coffee,' he said. 'Can I get one for you?'

'Yes please. Do they do proper coffee here?'

'I only live next door and I've brought in coffee and my cafetiere. Lottie doesn't mind me using the kitchen.'

He started to leave and she called him back.

'I don't quite understand what's going on, Alan. Lottie told me you arranged for me to be transferred here. Is that right?'

He looked awkward for a second then shrugged and smiled. 'Do you mind?' he asked.

'I'd like to know why.'

'I thought you'd be lonely. Your husband was clearly fixated on seeing the other flats...when I rang him, he asked if you were all right but he didn't even ask what sort of injuries you had.'

Louise turned away. Tears stung her eyes but she refused to cry. She knew Alan was telling the truth. It was par for the course with John. He liked to focus on one thing at a time. 'Coffee would be good right now,' she said.

Louise glanced out of the window. A male blackbird was sitting in the branch of a birch tree warbling its complex songs. It reminded her of a day walking with her father on the North Yorkshire moors, the year before he died. He was brilliant at whistling and liked to try and copy birdsong and sing it back to them. That day a bullfinch followed them for almost a mile, chirping back and forth with her father. It was a delicious day, full of potent plant scents, the musk of deer, the bullfinch and later, her father's arms holding her close as they parted at York railway station. The next time she saw him he was in a coma and three days later he died.

She met John the following year in the Lake District, at a weekend conference on Landscape and Literature. He was one of the speakers, the most charismatic of the three and he was very complimentary about her drawings, which were being exhibited at the same centre. Because John was her senior by ten years, her sister, Maddie, insisted that Louise was looking for a father substitute. There had been times over the last year when she thought Maddie might be right. But if she was going to move hundreds of miles to be with John, she decided she'd better be sure of her feelings...and his.

Alan returned with the coffee and some sandwiches on a tray.

'Might be good to eat something,' he said. 'They don't serve the evening meal here until six-thirty.'

Seeing the food, Louise realised how hungry she was. In between mouthfuls of tuna and cucumber, she surreptitiously watched Alan and found herself comparing him to John. It was a stupid thing to do because everything about Alan was new and therefore fresh. Familiarity had shone a bright light on her relationship with John. When Alan's mobile rang it startled them both.

'Hello?' he said. 'Yes...no, they're keeping her in overnight...' Louise reached out for the phone. She knew it was John. 'No, just hang on and I'll put Louise on.' Alan said. He fumbled with the phone and handed it to her.

'Hello? John? John?' She handed the phone back to Alan. 'He's gone,' she said. This time the tears slithered out and Alan rang for Lottie. When she came, he left the room, awkwardly carrying his mug of coffee.

Lottie held Louise in her arms and allowed her to cry herself out. When she finally flopped back onto the pillows, Lottie wiped her face with a cool cloth.

'You're still in shock, Louise and your husband probably thinks he's doing the right thing, taking care of the practical stuff. And in a way he's right isn't he? He can't do much to help you but he can get on with sorting the car and the accommodation.'

Louise told her about the farm and the argument they'd had and asked,

'How would you feel if it was your husband?'

Lottie looked away for a second before saying,

'I'd be hurt, just like you. But it's not the end of the world is it?'

Louise took a deep breath. There was no point dwelling on it but the fact was that John had become less interested in her since Amy had been born and he wasn't attached to the baby at all. Her mother had told her that all new fathers went through something similar.

'He'll come round when Amy starts talking and wanting him to play with her,' she'd added.

Lottie left and Alan returned. His eyes were sad but when he smiled at her she felt better. They talked quietly about his painting and her work as a graphic designer. His enthusiasm was catching and she told him her plans to set up her own business when Amy went to school.

'I'll do book design, greetings cards, posters for theatre,' she said. 'It'll be great fun and I'll be able to organise my time so that I'm there for Amy after school and in the holidays. When I was little both my parents had to work and I hated the after-school club because the worst bully in the school went to it.'

They were laughing when John strode into the room. His face was agitated and he paused, taking in the comfortable scene before walking up to the bed.

'John!' Louise said.

John leaned over the bed and kissed Louise on the cheek. When he straightened up he looked pointedly at Alan who'd remained seated.

'Do I know you?'

Alan pushed the chair back, stood up and held out his hand. He was a good few inches taller than John, who had to lean forward to shake hands.

'I'm Alan, PC Turner, we spoke on the phone.'

'Oh...' John said.

'Yes and he's been really kind,' Louise added.

The two men held eye contact, like a couple of dogs sizing one another up.

'Don't you have criminals to catch?' John asked.

'I'm off duty.'

John looked from Alan to Louise and back again. 'I'm sorry, am I missing something?' he said.

'He only lives next door,' said Louise, trying to dilute the tension.

'She was injured and she was alone in a strange place. Anyone would have done the same,' Alan said.

'Oh, would they?' John said. His tone was clipped and Louise tried to reach his hand to reassure him. 'You wouldn't like to put a little bet on that I suppose?' John continued. 'I mean the odds against a policeman taking someone from a road accident under his wing, even after he was off duty do seem stacked in my favour.'

Alan closed the distance between him and John by several inches.

'John, please. There's no need to be aggressive,' Louise said. 'Alan's been great. And as you didn't see fit to come, I'm very glad he was here.'

John turned back towards her. 'Yes, I'm sorry about that sweetheart. I thought you'd want me to sort everything out so that I had a car to pick you up and then I got cut off when I rang up here.' He paused, glanced at Alan and turned back to Louise.

'I thought you'd hung up on me,' she said. He stared at her bruised face for a few seconds before bending down to hold her. 'I'm really sorry. I should have come straight here, shouldn't I?' Louise nodded.

Alan started to walk away but Louise called him back. 'Alan, please don't go like this. I'm sure John didn't mean to...well, you know. He was worried.'

Alan stared at John, as if waiting for him to speak. When he didn't, Alan nodded and smiled. 'Well, now he can make up for lost time. Bye.'

John waited until Alan was out of the way before speaking. 'What a creep! Hanging around you like that.'

Louise sighed and it quickly turned into a long, noisy yawn. John glanced at his watch.

'Will they let you out of here tonight?' he asked.

'They said tomorrow morning.'

'All right, I'll let you sleep then. You need to build up your energy reserves and I've got a few more flats to see.'

And then he was gone and despite her tiredness, Louise felt like he'd taken all the warmth of the room away with him. She was soon asleep and woke to the aroma of curry. It was a favourite of hers but she wasn't hungry. Lottie took the dinner off her tray and handed it back to the orderly.

'Your husband's been on the phone,' she said. 'He asked me to tell you that he's found the perfect flat, near a park but not far from the city centre or the university.'

'Thank you,' Louise said, unable to hide her disappointment.

'Oh,' Lottie said, handing her an envelope. 'I nearly forgot. Alan left this for you.'

Lottie left the room and Louise carefully opened the envelope. It was a small watercolour made into a card. It had the purple hills in the background and in the foreground a farmer and two dogs were taking their cows in for milking. She could just make out a thatched roof in the distance and wondered if it could possibly be the farm she and John had viewed that morning. When she opened the card she was stunned. It said,

*Leave your husband and come and live with me.
He doesn't appreciate you. You can have your place in
the wilds and I will love your daughter as if she was my
own and help you with your plans. Alan.*

She dropped the card on the bed and lay quietly
with her eyes closed for some time but her skin was
molten. She was drained but she was angry that Alan saw
her as something to be passed between men, as if she was
unable to make decisions for herself. But when she
thought about it, maybe that was the impression she'd
given him about the farm cottage, that John was the one
in charge. She wanted to live on that farm but she'd
succumbed to pressure from him. She turned and stared
out of the window and there on the branch of a tree sat a
magnificent bullfinch. Every hair on her body stood on
end. She sat up and rang for a nurse. Lottie came in.

'Can I get hold of a phone please?' Louise asked.

'Of course you can. Here use my mobile.'

Lottie handed it to her and walked away. John's
phone went to voicemail. Louise was quick and precise.

*John, I want us to live in the farm cottage,
otherwise I'll reconsider moving to Devon. I don't want
to discuss it any further. This move is for your benefit
and I want things to be right for Amy and me as well.
Just text yes or no.*

It was a test. But Louise knew she might not have
been focussed enough to give such an ultimatum without
Alan's strange proposal. John replied within a few
minutes.

*Yes darling, you're right. I've been totally
pigheaded as usual. I'll see to it now.*

Lottie arrived to pick up her phone. 'You look a
bit brighter,' she said.

Louise nodded. 'Yes, I've been very decisive. It
feels good.'

Lottie stood there with a question in her eyes.

'I've told John I want to live at the farm and he's
agreed.'

'That's brilliant, I hope it works out.'

Lottie started to leave but Louise picked up Alan's card and called her back. 'Would you return this to Alan for me?' She asked. 'I don't think I should see him again before I leave.' Lottie paused at the end of the bed and glanced at the card, inside and out.

'I think you've made the right decision,' she said.

'Thanks, but tell me why.'

'Sure you want to know?'

'Absolutely.'

'Alan falls in and out of love all the time.'

'Ah, the voice of experience.'

'Some young nurses had to learn a hard lesson.'

'Well I'm very grateful for his...intervention.'

Lottie laughed and left Louise to rest.

The following day John drove them back to Yorkshire with a contract for the farm cottage in his pocket. Louise stretched out on the back seat of the car with a blanket over her. He drove with care and they were mostly wrapped up in their own thoughts. At one point Louise leaned forward and squeezed his arm. Through the driving mirror he smiled and blew her a kiss. Something between them had changed, lifted.

The Bones of Saint Ignatious

FATHER KERRIGAN WOULD HAVE BET THE BONES OF SAINT
Ignatious that he would only ever in his life hear a single
confession like the one Alice Noonan had made to him
several years before. The particular subject of the
confession hadn't come up during his training and he was
woefully ill equipped to deal with it. After he'd given her
Absolution for her sins, she asked if he had any advice he
could offer about her 'situation'. He was so disorientated,
he told her the story of a village that lapped the edges of
the Pacific Ocean and used the hairs of the yak to fortify
buildings against the pitiless advance of the sea.

'Is there a moral for me in the story, Father?'
Alice Noonan had asked and in his desperation to offer
help, he told her that when she unravelled the moral she'd
find a solution to her problem.

He remembered the incident as if it had
happened barely a week since and then only a month ago,
hadn't he heard the self-same problem revealed once
more in the secrecy of the confessional. How could his
small parish be so cursed, he asked his Maker. One
person's curse is another person's blessing, his Maker
answered, enigmatic as usual.

Alice Noonan owned a boggy bit of land halfway down the
valley between the Quinlan and Riley farms. It wasn't

large enough to pursue a good living and the water from the pump in Quinlan's field was awful bitter and scaly, so she worked a couple of days a week skelping the fractious hens which belonged to Rody Riley.

Alice could turn crops with the best of them, and sometimes did when the hen work was scarce but what Rody really valued was her cooking. Each week she'd bring a slice of tart, a scone or some such thing, for his tea break. His wife, Enda, had what they called sour fingers; any shred of fresh food she touched grew fur. A look from her was enough some days. Alice Noonan secretly thought that Enda had been weaned on the Black Lake water below Snake Pass, for she was a wise lady of leisure since she'd hooked Rody with her pinched-in waists and the promise of dangerous pleasures, which apparently never materialised.

Alice Noonan lived alone. Not that she hadn't had proposals of marriage you understand; virtually every bachelor within three counties, without a mammy at home, had got down on his knee to her at one time or another. Nor was she nursing a broken heart from some disastrous past love affair. But she made it abundantly clear, to anyone who cared to ask, that she preferred to live on her own.

The lads who propped up the bar at the Beehive five or six nights a week spent many an hour speculating about Alice Noonan's desires. And this night I'm talking about, a month after Father Kerrigan's second big confessional shock, was no exception.

Laurence Dolan, Tommy Prendergast and Jimmy Conlin were waiting for Mick Nugent, the latest member of their card squad, to arrive, so when Father Kerrigan came in they were pleased to draw him into their conversation. They let him down two pints with chasers, on top of a double malt, before attempting to get him talking.

'I'd say he didn't have much of a start in life now, wouldn't you agree Father?' Laurence Dolan began in his usual laconic fashion.

'Nor did any of us if I'm not mistaken,' Tommy Prendergast put in.

'Ah, but we all knew who our father was, isn't that the case?' Dolan replied.

'Only if our mothers are to be believed,' Jimmy Conlin said in his half-hearted way.

It was a warm September evening that promised thunder later. Clouds edged with purple were scudding their way speedily over the hilltops.

'Alice was wild with rage wasn't she Father?' Laurence Dolan tried again.

'I'd say she had every right to be so,' Father Kerrigan responded curtly.

'If she could have got her hands on Paddy Kelly he'd have been rashers, no doubt about that,' Dolan continued.

'She ran after him over four fields with Scully's axe in her hand,' Jimmy Conlin added. 'He had to chance Phelan's bull to get away from her.'

'Ah well, give me Phelan's bull any day over Alice in a lather,' said Prendergast, watching the priest out of the corner of his watery eye. 'What d'you say Father?'

Father Kerrigan ignored him and banged his glass on the counter, signifying he was ready for more alcohol. The barman wearily shook his head, knowing he'd have to drag the priest out of the pub later and drive him home, yet again.

'She's a fine woman all the same,' Dolan said.

'Will she never marry?' Conlin added. 'I hear she's had endless proposals.'

'She says she won't,' Prendergast answered. 'It seems she can't have children and she says that's the only good reason she can think of for marrying. Though I myself can think of a few more.'

'Did she tell you that herself, about not having children?' Conlin asked.

'No, I met Brid Doherty at the market and she has

a sister who's married to the cousin of a fella who lives on the edge of Quinlan's land and he had the story.'

'Sure what harm,' the barman chipped in.

'What harm indeed,' Conlin agreed.

'Mind, I'd be lonely I'd say,' Dolan ventured.

'You'd be lonely in a crowd, Dolan and frequently are,' Father Kerrigan snapped.

'That's true enough,' Prendergast added, with no intention of malice.

Paddy Kelly had taken the bet — that he couldn't get a photograph of Alice Noonan in the pelt — without blinking an eye. They'd all chipped in, Dolan, Prendergast, Conlin and Nugent, ten pounds each. He'd borrowed the barman's camera, which had a telephoto lens and waited patiently on top of the bales of hay in her barn until he'd seen the light go on in her ground floor bathroom. He knew, from years past, that there was a short corridor between the bathroom and the stairs up to the bedroom and that through the plain glass in her back door this corridor could be clearly seen.

His vantage point in the barn was only a matter of a couple of metres from the house and he was comfortable, leaning on the hay and swallowing the occasional mouthful of whisky from his flask. But still Alice took him by surprise when she did walk stark naked along the corridor towards the door with just a small towel around her hair. He was so startled he dropped the camera on to the concrete floor of the barn with an almighty clatter. Alice couldn't see who was outside but she certainly heard the noise. Donning boots and a large overcoat she came after him like a mad sow with a fresh litter, waving Scully's old axe in front of her. Kelly escaped with cuts and bruises but he was still paying back the barman for his damaged camera.

'What could have driven Paddy to give up the cards and drink Father?' Dolan asked. Father Kerrigan banged his empty glass down on the counter and ignored the question.

'T'was the fear,' Jimmy Conlin offered, 'being pursued by an axe and driven into the arms of a bull. That's enough to curdle the brains of any man, surely.'

'Comprehensively,' Prendergast said. He was the man for the words and always carried a small dictionary in his pocket to assist him in extending his vocabulary.

Dolan and Conlin exchanged anxious looks. Dolan had heard a rumour once about a farmhand further east who'd been caught with his joystick up the arse of a Friesian cow.

'Not a bull, that would be suicide,' Conlin said.

'Everything that is on this Earth is of God's making, don't you understand that yet?' Father Kerrigan shouted.

'Of course Father, of course,' Dolan replied. 'Here, let me get you another drink. Sure a priest should never be without a drink after a hard day's work, should he lads?'

'Not at all, not at all,' the lads agreed.

'Where's Mick got himself to?' Prendergast asked. 'Look at the time, will you. He's not a patch on Paddy for punctuality. There'll hardly be chance for half a dozen games at this rate.'

The barman refilled the priest's glasses and hoped that the Lord God Almighty was appreciative of what he did for the auld fella and would maybe throw a bit of extra Grace his way.

'Could Paddy have found a woman?' Jimmy Conlin said into the comfortable silence. A log suddenly fell out of the fireplace and crashed onto the floorboards and there were those who would later say that it was a sort of omen.

'And who would it be that we wouldn't know about it?' Dolan answered and then lowered his voice and glanced around the room. 'In fact many of his friends were worried that he might be a homosexual underneath it all.'

'*Homo*sexual, you dolt!' Father Kerrigan shouted. 'Keep digging Dolan. You've tried bestiality, now homosexuality, what's to be next?'

'I beg your pardon Father but I've never tried either of those 'alities', if you don't mind,' Dolan said with a wink to the others. As they'd discovered many times before, Father Kerrigan revealed most when he was drunk and angry.

As the priest opened his mouth to speak, Mick Nugent tore into the bar like a man possessed. He tapped on the counter in his characteristic way, demanding a pint, while he fought his laboured breathing.

'Jesus!' he said eventually. 'Jesus! Excuse me father but 'tis the only word for it.'

'What, man?' Dolan asked, his curiosity making his left leg twitch. 'What is it that's making you curse in front of the priest?'

Nugent was still breathing hard as Prendergast and Conlin crowded in on him, all demanding an explanation.

'Alice Noonan and Paddy Kelly,' he said breathlessly, creating silence in the room. Everyone waited for the rest of the sentence. 'In the river, in the moonlight, bare as a bald man's head. Dancing and singing like two nightingales. And both of them...'

Nugent stopped there and glanced at the priest who was suddenly smiling like an inebriated cherub. For he had broken his confessional vow and phoned Alice Noonan two night's back to tell her she had another like herself in his parish, and that yaks were thought to be bisexual.

'If they were in the river, naked as peeled onions then they've lost the right to privacy,' Prendergast said indignantly. At which Father Kerrigan started laughing so loudly that he fell backwards off his stool and knocked himself out on the wooden floor. For once the barman didn't rush to his aid. He too was hanging on Mick Nugent's words. It was only the excess of drink, conveniently keeping his limbs supple, which prevented the priest from being badly injured.

'Go on Mick, tell the tale, God's representative is no longer listening,' Dolan said.

'Both of them,' Nugent said again, pausing for greater effect, because he knew full well he had everyone's attention, 'both of them with breasts and plonkers!'

The communal gasp that issued from the lips of the assembled men could have filled a flagging sail.

'Hermaphrodites!' Prendergast said into the space, for after all he was the man who had the words.

'Lucky sods...lucky, lucky sods,' said Conlin and all the lads nodded their agreement.

In the stunned silence that followed, all that could be heard was the cracking of the logs on the fire and Father Kerrigan's legendary snores.

Hunted

IT BEGAN DURING THE SUMMER HOLIDAYS THAT I WAS TWELVE. Dad had suddenly been made redundant, along with a load of other skilled steel workers. Up until the last minute, it looked like the company was going to get away with a pitiful settlement. Then, in response to an appeal with thousands of signatures, which dad had sent to his MP, things changed. The guy came up and joined the picket line and that's where I met him. Mam had sent me with some food for the lads and dad introduced me to him. There was something about the way he looked at me — like a dog at his dinner — that disturbed my young, impressionable mind. But, he supported the strikers, had meetings in London and at the works and a good deal was swiftly negotiated.

After that, dad volunteered to work for him and he had me helping out with delivering party leaflets, door-to-door stuff, after school and at weekends. I was fed up because my mate, Rob and me had just got into go-kart racing and we were building a super kart in his gran's shed.

One Saturday I went to the constituency office to take dad some lunch and found him licking this MP guy's boots. When I walked in the guy's eyes glittered, like they had on the picket line. He was wearing expensive clothes, his hair had been blow-dried and his watch was top of the range. Round where we lived – with half the dads on the dole – that was regarded as class: the class that doesn't have to toil for a living. But in dad's books, his MP could do no wrong.

After I'd handed over his sandwiches, dad tried to get me delivering the monthly newsletter. I told him Rob was waiting for me. You don't cross my dad though; he's an ex-amateur boxer and ready to go a few rounds with anyone. But Mr High-up read my expression and took my side.

'The lad's got to have some fun, Larry,' he said. 'I'll drop him off on my way to the meeting.'

Dad agreed but gave me a look that threatened retaliation.

When we got to high-up's car my eyes saucered; he had a brand new BMW, deep blue with glittering chrome. I clambered into the passenger seat, breathing in the lush smell of quality leather.

'Nice?' he asked. I nodded enthusiastically. 'Like to go for quick drive before I drop you at your pal's?'

I nodded, that was more like it. 'Can we go up the motorway, fast as you can?' I asked.

'Strap up then,' he replied, letting his left hand rest on to my knee for a second.

He removed it while he got the car into gear and manoeuvred it around the town, but once on the motorway his hand returned to my knee and stayed. I didn't know what to do or say. I was uncomfortable but he wasn't actually hurting me. Was my knee a private part? Dad's attempt at sexual education was telling me: *if anyone tries to touch your private parts you tell me, sharpish.*

Out of the corner of my eye I watched his face. There was just that set smile I'd seen in so many newspaper photos. The speedo climbed up and up until we were doing a hundred and twenty miles an hour and him driving with one hand. I'd never gone so fast and began laughing with the thrill of it. He moved his hand further up my thigh, pausing only centimetres from my balls. I stopped laughing and moved his hand. He glanced at me, something like a cobra might before it strikes.

'Sorry,' he said but he put his hand back on my knee for the return journey.

I was nervous so I gabbled, told him all about Rob and our super-kart plans and he just smiled. When he pulled up at the end of Rob's gran's street, he said,

'I grew up round here and I know you can make it big in this world if you meet the right people, otherwise it's the shit heap.'

I started to get out of the car and he handed me a tenner. I must have looked at him strangely because as I walked past his window he opened it and said,

'That's to help with the go-kart. I'll see you again soon.'

Rob sat popeyed while I told him about...let's call him, Roger.

'He was making you an offer,' he said when I'd finished.

'Think so?'

'Yeah, all that, making it big if you know the right people: that was an offer.'

'In exchange for my backside? No thanks.'

Rob nearly choked himself laughing. Then we got on with the go-kart building. I forgot about everything else and was late home for tea.

'You're getting a bit cocky for my liking,' dad said as I sat down at the table. Mam smiled at me over the top of his head and got my food out of the oven. 'First you show me up in front of Roger and then you're late for your tea.'

I didn't respond. Dad reacts better to silence than back chat.

'I thought Roger said he was a charming lad,' mam chipped in.

She could get away with it. As far as dad was concerned, he had married an angel and I wasn't going to start arguing with that.

As I started eating my shepherd's pie, dad said,

'Tomorrow, Roger wants you to help him out with his constituency work.' I glanced at mum and she raised her eyebrows. 'He thinks you'll go down well with the punters, door to door. Especially those that are dithering about voting for him. You're a local lad, all that stuff.'

'He told me he came from round here,' I said.

'Not this end of town pet,' mam said. 'He's from the posh quarter.'

'His father was a self-made man,' dad added.

'Was he now? Pat Connely says different.'

'Pat Connely, Irish-ex-communist-party-hack wants to watch his tongue.'

I finished my food quickly and stood up. This was familiar territory. Pat was married to my aunt Jane, mam's sister, and dad had never liked him. As I reached the hall door he was well into his commie-bashing routine but he paused to shout at me.

'You'll be coming into the office with me at 9.30 in the morning. You can stamp some envelopes until Roger arrives at ten.'

I nodded and ran up the stairs before he could say anything else. I texted Rob and said I couldn't get until the afternoon. He texted me,

Watch yer back

Next morning, mam had sandwiches and flasks made up for me and dad and a bacon butty ready to eat on the way. She looked hung over. I guessed she'd been on the gin after I went to bed. It was her weakness but dad ignored it because his angel could do no wrong.

'Dad's agreed that you can go to Rob's after two,' she whispered. 'Best I could do, pal.'

I hugged her and followed him out to his battered Fiesta, hoping that it wouldn't start, which was a fairly regular event. It kicked in at the third turn of the ignition. By the time Roger arrived at the office, my mouth was sore with licking envelope gum. He and dad had a chat in the reception area and I poured a coffee out of my flask. It was perfect, strong and milky.

'Well then Colin,' Roger said as he followed dad into the room. 'Let's go and canvass some votes.'

I followed him out of the office, downstairs and into the street. Once in the car I told Roger I was expected back at two.

'No problem.'

We did about 20 streets before Roger turned to me and said,

'I'm fed up of pressing the flesh. Let's go for a spin.'

I thought about refusing but we were right out at the edge of his constituency and I had no idea how to get back home. This time he went south on the motorway. He took the speedo up to one thirty and again, rested his hand on my knee. As the clock edged up towards one forty-five I closed my eyes in excited terror. Roger's hand moved upwards and then he tried to undo my flies. I pushed him away and moved right up against the car door. He laughed and put his hand back on the steering wheel. Fifteen minutes later, as we drew up near Rob's gran's, he said,

'Best not tell your dad we were joyriding instead of working. He wouldn't like it,' and he handed me another tenner.

Things went on like that for a month. Whenever he was in the constituency, he'd be on my case. Every so often he'd ask me get my prick out and I'd refuse. It made me think I had some control over his actions and each tenner he gave me contributed to the go-kart building scheme. Rob was the only one I told.

'He's biding his time, man,' Rob said. 'That's what thi do...it's called grooming. Colin, I'm warning yer, kick him into touch.'

But I couldn't tell dad I didn't want to see Roger, unless I was prepared to tell him everything. And y'know what? He wouldn't have believed me anyway. Roger had

looked after him when the steelworks closed and Roger
had got him cash-in-hand work at the constituency office.
Maybe Roger thought I was his payback.

One day, Rob's brother Jed came into his gran's
shed while we were working on the go-kart. He was in the
army and on leave from Afghanistan. He stood in the
doorway and stared at us for ages without speaking, until
Rob said,

'What's the score, Jed?'

'This is my hangout,' he said. His voice was more
a growl.

'Not any more mate; you've got the big bedroom
at home, even when you're away. Yer can't stretch yer
arms out in mine without touching a wall. Fair's fair.'

'Hey Spud, don't talk t'me about fairness. I live in
a world where there's no such word. Right?' He sat down
in the corner.

'Right, man,' Rob said. 'That's cool but don't keep
calling me Spud.'

Jed laughed but it got strangled in his throat and
sounded like any angry dog. He got his tackle out and
rolled a huge, skunky spliff but when he got his lighter
out, Rob said,

'Not in here pal, we've got sweet, pink lungs and
we don't want your crap in them.' Rob's Granddad and
dad had died of lung cancer and he was rabidly anti-
smoking.

Jed compromised by standing in the doorway,
mumbling angrily to himself the whole time. Rob kept
making gestures about Jed being fucked up. When he
came back in, he sat down again and dropped his head
into his hands.

'No bugger talks about it any more,' he said. 'It's
all Arab Spring crap now.' He pointed a finger at us.
'There's US troops – or should I say mercenaries – on the
ground in every location that hits the news...and us, we
have to clean up the friggin' mess. Covert ops everywhere
man. I'm telling yer, it's shit. And our government right in

the middle of it and lying just like the other lot did about Iraq. There'd be a bloody revolution here if people knew the truth; if they were *told* the truth.'

I think Rob was trying to sidetrack him when he asked,

'Know anything about these wealthy guys who groom youngsters, Jed?'

'They don't have to do any grooming in a war zone, pal; there's guys out there all the time picking up kids who've lost their parents or can't find them. They've got private planes and helicopters. It's shit, I've told you, this world is going down the plughole.'

Even though I was nudging him, Rob went on,

'But what would you do if you found out about one grooming kids round here?'

'I'd chop his dick off.' He laughed and patted Rob on the back and for a moment, something of the old Jed flickered in his eyes: the guy we'd all looked up to, the football hero, the one who always pulled the women. Rob kept staring at me, trying to encourage me to tell Jed about Roger but I was too scared of what Jed might do and of what my dad might do.

Rob hadn't told me much of what had gone on with Jed, only that when he was fighting in Iraq and Afghanistan he was given free drugs and drink to help him through, just like all his pals and that he'd lost two good mates: one to so-called 'friendly fire', the other to a suicide bomber.

The last time Jed came home, I'd asked Rob, 'Why does he keep going back? Why doesn't he just go AWOL?'

'He's totally fucked up. Can't sleep without gruesome nightmares. Can't wake up without drugs, which he can't afford to buy over here. He lives on adrenalin now and over there, it's on tap twenty-four hours a day. That's what he told me.'

We ignored Jed and carried on with our painting. We'd decided to use our football team colours. Jed's spark soon faded, until he was like a balloon without enough air. When he finally left the shed, Rob had a go at me for not coming clean about Roger.

'You're out of your depth, Colin. This guy's an MP. He's been around the houses a few times and he's got contacts in high places.'

I was young but I wasn't stupid. Roger was a man who was used to getting his own way and had the sort of money that could buy what he wanted. I knew what he wanted from me but I thought I could keep him at bay without having to tell dad.

'Yeah but him being an MP makes him vulnerable, doesn't it?' I said. 'He wouldn't want the papers and TV to know what he's up to, would he?'

'You're so wrong pal. My mam says they all scratch one another's backs. The papers won't publish anything that affects their friends, or high-ups. You're the one that'll be up the river without a paddle. Step away now. It's been going on too long and every time you get in his car again, he takes that as you agreeing to his dirty tricks. Listen, I'll talk to our Jed if you want, he'll know what to do.'

'Not yet.'

I didn't listen to Rob because I had this plan. Next time dad told me Roger was coming, I borrowed my cousin Elisa's DAT machine. She had pretensions to be a top class journalist and used it to record things she saw when she was out and about.

'You've got to be ahead of the game,' she always told me. 'The only way is up and that's where I'm heading.'

She was sixteen going on sixty and she'd watched too many episodes of *Friends* and taken Joey as her role model. I kept trying to tell her that he was the main comic relief in the show but she wouldn't have it. Anyway, the machine was small enough to fit into my jacket pocket and best of all it was voice-activated. I bought brand new batteries and a pack of mini discs. By the time I arrived with dad's lunch the following day I was all set up. Roger was already there. His eyes lit up when he saw me. Dad was oblivious, so when Roger asked,

'Mind if I borrow him for a few hours?' Dad took it as a compliment.

On the way to his car Roger texted someone and I texted Rob: *game on.* Roger didn't ask me where I wanted to go and he still put his hand on my knee. When it started to creep up my thigh I moved my legs further away.

'You're a bit of a tease are you?' he said. 'I like that.'

I quickly realised that I had to start talking, otherwise the DAT would only record his voice. 'I'm not a tease and don't like you putting your hand on my knee,' I said.

He slowed suddenly at a traffic light and turned to look at me full on. His eyes were pale and his skin was too smooth for a man his age. I had an Uncle Mark who was a tranny and his skin was the same; he'd had some sort of electric treatment. Dad never talked about Mark. He had narrow horizons, my dad.

'Don't play silly buggers with me,' Roger said. It was the first time I'd felt really frightened of him. His face had morphed into something reptilian and dangerous.

'I'd like to go back now,' I said.

'Not yet, I've got a treat for you,' he said, stroking my thigh.

I was anxious when he pulled into the drive of a big house in the posh area of the city. 'Is this your house?' I asked.

He shook his head. 'Belongs to a friend.'

'What's this street called?' I asked, as we got out of the car.

'What's it to you?' he snapped and I stopped asking questions.

The front door swung open. The guy who stood there was broad and bulky, like some SAS type. He nodded at Roger. 'First floor, back room,' he told him.

As we reached the first floor my guts were churning.

'I need the toilet,' I said.

Roger guided me to a small lavatory and stood there with the door open while I peed. Then he led me along the corridor and opened the door to a massive room, which was in semi-darkness. There was a large screen on the wall and at first I couldn't work out what I was seeing. Roger pushed me over to a large sofa, where another man was sitting with a lad of about my age. He looked at me, his eyes full of trouble. I sat and looked at the screen again. At first I thought it was men and young women having sex, then I realised it was men having sex with young boys. The full of horror of what Roger was about hit me like a well-packed snowball.

I stood up and tried to get to the door but Roger pulled me back. I fought him off and started shouting. The big guy came running in and slapped me.

'Stay there and stay quiet until Roger says it's time to go, or I'll really hurt you,' he said.

I sat still and looked down at my knees but the sound effects on the film still made me feel ill. I hoped the DAT machine was picking it all up. About half an hour later, the other guy switched the screen off and said to Roger,

'Come and see what I brought back from Thailand.' Roger nodded at us. 'They'll be fine, Billy's outside the door.'

They went through to an adjoining room and I looked at the lad next to me.

'You'll get used to it,' he whispered, 'just think of something else. Which Home you in?'

'I'm not, I live with mam and dad.'

'Don't tell them,' he said. 'That's how I ended up in Barnardo's. It was our doctor what groomed me and when I told my mam and dad he said I'd tried to get money off him and he'd refused and now I was getting

back at him. My parents believed him. Hey man, it's
better than being on street corners and he won't fuck you
straight away; Roger likes the chase.'

Roger and the guy came back. I'd decided I'd say
nothing. I just wanted him to drop me off without...doing
that stuff to me. When he hit the main road and put his
hand on my prick I started crying, I couldn't help it.

'It's all right,' he said. 'Now you know the score.'
He pulled into a dark side street and wiped my face with
his hanky. The car doors were locked and when he
unzipped his flies, I thought I'd pass out. 'It's all right. I
just need to...do this...'

I closed my eyes tight and when he moaned and
flopped back on his seat, I knew he'd finished. 'See, that
wasn't too bad, was it?' he said as he cleaned himself with
baby wipes. I stared at the window.

'Rob'll be wondering where I am,' I said. My
throat was so tight it came out hoarse.

'Well, we'd better get going then.'

I sank into a dark pit until I started recognising
the streets. He pulled in on the corner near Rob's gran's
and unlocked the doors. As I climbed out he said,

'Take a look in the boot.'

As I got to the rear of the car, he released the
lock. Inside the boot was a top of the range, racing go-
kart. I leaned down to check it out and when I stood up he
was beside me. Shielded by the car and the boot, he took
my hand and pressed it onto his trousers and his erect
prick. I let out a cry and jumped free of him. As I started
to walk away he called after me.

'Haven't you forgotten something?' When I
turned round the go-kart was on the pavement. 'This is
for you,' he called out.

When I look back, I know that was the pivotal
moment, the point of corruption. If I took the kart, he
would see it as acquiescence. But it was so magnificent
and so out of Rob's reach and mine, I couldn't resist.

'I'll see you soon,' he said. Then he was gone,

gliding off in his fancy machine.

I shouted Rob as I was walking down the path; he poked his head out of the shed, saw the kart and sprinted up to me.

'Omigod...omigod,' he kept saying. Then he looked at me, went silent, and took hold of my arms.

'It's from him isn't it?' I nodded. 'What did you do Colin? You didn't let him—'

'No,' I shouted.

We went into the shed and I rewound the tape and played it. Rob sat rigid while we listened. 'Ferkin' hell, Colin...you've got to get out of this...I'm not sure you've got enough on here to go to the police. The only person who calls him by name, and that's his first name, is the bodyguard guy. They'd probably have to get a voice recognition expert in. Would they do that? Plus there's a lot of interference. But let's play it for Jed, see what he thinks.'

'But what if he wants to tell dad? He'd slaughter me.'

'I'll come with you. I'll be there while you tell Jed.'

'But it's my fault. I...I should have run off that first time and told mam then. But...I...' I started crying again.

Jed suddenly stumbled into the shed. He was totally out of it and fell on top of Rob. I had to help lift him off. We rolled him into the corner on top of an old rug. In between snoring and tossing about he kept shouting out orders like,

'Run...down this way, quick...no...don't...fuck...'

'It's like he's got a nightmare on a loop in his head,' Rob said. 'I've heard it loads of times.' He grabbed my arm. 'Now you listen to me, when he's sober we've got to tell him about Roger, he's the only one who can help us.'

'Please Rob, give us a few days, I'll try and talk to mam.'

'If you can catch her sober.'

My eyes filled up again and he punched me on the arm. 'Come on; let's take this cracker of a kart out for a spin, up on West Works Hill and see what it's made of?'

He was only trying to cheer me up but I shook my head. 'I don't want to touch it,' I said. 'I'll give it back.'

He nodded.

I thought it would be a few weeks before I saw Roger again. Time enough for me to build up the courage to speak to mam. I secretly hoped he'd finished with me, and the go-kart was the price of my silence. But next morning at breakfast dad said,

'Roger's got a big job for you today: some door to door and some meetings at community centres.'

I glanced at mam and she picked up that I wasn't happy. 'Does he have to go? I think he looks like he's coming down with something,' she said.

Dad stared at me. 'Don't you want to help Roger?' he said.

I shook my head, 'Not really...I— '

'Not really!' he shouted. 'After all he's done for this family?'

He stood up and started banging about, knocking ornaments off the shelves and kicking furniture. I thought mam might be next.

'All right! All right! I'll do it,' I shouted.

'Of course you'll bloody do it. Go and get in the car.'

I picked up my jacket and remembered I'd left the DAT machine in the shed at Rob's granny's. Mam was cowering in the corner of the kitchen and dad was still stomping about.

'Don't you hit her,' I said to him. I felt unstable. The thought of what Roger might do to me was sending my head into a spin.

'Since when did you tell me what to do?' he growled.

The doorbell rang and mam almost ran to answer it. Dad and me stood there eyeballing each other. I think he knew that for the first time in my life I wasn't going to back down.

Mam led Rob and Jed into the kitchen. Rob nodded at me.

'All right Mr Parker,' he said to dad.

'I'm fine,' he replied before saying, 'Jed?'

'Mr Parker.'

There was a bulky silence, broken by mum a few seconds later. 'Jed's taking the lads to the go-kart track today,' she said. 'I'm sorry, I forgot all about it.'

Dad brushed past me and picked up his coat.

'He's got work to do, canvassing.'

'Roger can do without him for one day, can't he?' Mum said.

'No, he's not letting Roger down.'

'I'm only on leave for another week Mr Parker, want to give 'em a treat before I go back,' Jed said; his fists clenched and unclenched as he spoke. Rob glanced at me and his eyes were jumpy.

'The track racing's on tomorrow,' dad said. 'You can take him then.'

For a second, I thought Jed was going to implode. His eyes seemed to tremble and show too much white but something pulled him back. 'Mr Parker...I'm shocked you're still canvassing for Labour after everything that lot did to the country,' he said, coldly. 'Come on Rob, we'll see Colin later.' Mam showed them to the door.

I knew, from the look Jed gave me, that Rob had played the tape to him. But he still had an honour code of his own: he wouldn't spill the beans to mam and dad without my say so. When they'd gone it was like I was looking down a black hole with no way out. I followed dad to the car, neither of us spoke a word until we were inside the constituency office.

'Get those leaflets into envelopes while you're waiting,' he said, before going into his office. I thought about running back home, or over to Rob's but I knew dad would be like a mad bull and more than me would suffer. Half an hour later, Roger arrived. He whistled as he came up the stairs, *Dancing Queen* by Abba. I made up my mind that I was going to stand up to him before everything got totally out of control.

In the car, he made no pretence of going canvassing. He headed straight for the motorway. He didn't even put his hand on my knee. A tiny part of me cheered, perhaps he had done with me. But when he turned off onto a small road, my stomach jumped.

'Where are you taking me?' I asked.

He laughed. It reminded me of a shed full of turkeys.

'My friends and I like sharing our new conquests.'

We were in the countryside by that time and I hadn't been paying attention. I wasn't sure where he'd turned off the motorway. He was driving too fast for me to consider jumping out and besides the doors were always locked.

'I don't want to meet your friends,' I said. 'Take me back or I'll tell my dad about you.'

'No you won't,' Roger said, 'and anyway, who do you think he'd believe? Me or you?'

A few miles on he turned into a long driveway with steep hedges close in on either side. Not ideal running away territory. As the drive widened I saw a large detached house with several expensive cars parked in front of it. Beside each car stood a large man looking like they were extras in some Rambo film.

As Roger slowed to park, I got ready to run. I planned to go cross-country so that I couldn't be followed by car. When he stopped and turned the engine off, he climbed out without even looking at me. I let him walk a few paces towards the house before I tried to open the door on my side. It was still locked. I scrambled over to the driver's side but as I did, one of the bulky men climbed in. It was the guy who'd been at the big house and I knew he'd hit me if I didn't co-operate.

'I want to get out,' I said.

'Too late for that mate,' he replied.

'It's not. Who are you?'

'We're the dogsbodies but the pay's good. Give me your mobile and don't tell me you haven't got one.'

'I haven't got it with me,' I said as my stomach filled with broken glass. He leant over and roughly checked my pockets. I was glad I hadn't got the DAT machine.

'Let me guess,' he said. 'You've had money and probably an expensive gift from Roger and you thought it was all for nothing? Pull the other one kid.'

'My dad's gonna kill you when I tell him!' I yelled. He laughed.

'Roger always has things covered, nobody will believe you and he'll have a cast iron alibi with several respectable witnesses.' He nodded his head. 'That's right kid, but don't worry; they get bored of you when you hit sixteen.'

I leaned back on my seat, shaking and terrified.

'Just let me go. Why can't you let me go?' I pleaded.

'This is what I get paid for, pal. I'd be out of a job and out of a life. These guys don't get caught because some nobody or other takes the blame. Money and influence, no point in fighting it. Now take off your jeans and pants.'

'No.'

'You want me to drag them off you?'

I shook my head.

'Right then, jeans and pants o—'

He didn't have time to finish his sentence before Jed and another guy in army fatigues pulled him out of the car, and dragged him along the gravel. Rob leaned in and grabbed my hand and we ran down the drive. As we reached the bend I glanced back and saw eight or nine more guys in army fatigues following Jed and his mate.

Two of them were filming everything. Round the corner, Rob led me to where six cars and two motorbikes were parked.

'You saved my life,' I told him.

'It was Jed. When your dad said Roger was coming for you, he knew he had to do something. The minute we left you he started ringing round. He always has fatigues and a weapon in the boot of his car, says it's the only thing that makes him feel safe.'

'You followed us.'

'Yep, just like a bloody film; they kept swapping places so that Roger wouldn't twig. I played your tape to Jed.'

'I thought you had.'

'When it had finished he said: *Is that who I think it is?* And when I nodded he started ranting: *That bastard. It was him and his pals that got us into Iraq and while we're having our heads kicked in, he's over here fucking underage kids.*'

Half an hour later, Jed and some of his mates came back with the other young lads, fully dressed. The lads got in one of the other cars and Jed leaned in our window.

'Gary's going to drop you two off. My pals and me are going to have a serious talk with Roger and his friends. See you later.'

Gary was the silent type but like Jed he kept up a quiet monologue with himself all the way back to Jed's gran's. Rob and me tried to work on the go-kart but every time there was noise outside we jumped. I was so much on edge I sliced into my hand with a screwdriver. Jed took me into his gran and she cleaned it up and put a plaster on. Rob made two mugs of tea to take back with us. Jed was sitting in the corner of the shed when we got there.

'Thanks Jed,' I said.

'Believe me, it was a pleasure.'

We waited for him to say more but he said

nothing and then started rolling a spliff.

'What's the deal man?' Rob asked. 'Will he go to prison or what?'

He shook his head. 'I told yer, this country's gone to the dogs,' he said. 'Gary's been on to all the news agencies over here but nobody'll touch the film. He put a section on YouTube and it was removed within minutes. It never even got loaded on Facebook. So much for social media creating a new democracy. The guy who created Facebook worked for the CIA. That's all you need to know. Remember that when you see stuff on the web. Gary's trying some of the foreign news agencies now. Maybe Iran will pick it up,' Rob said.

'What about the other lads?' I asked.

'All from Care Homes,' Jed said. 'We gave them a choice about whether they wanted to speak out. None of them did. I'm sure you can imagine some of the reasons why.'

'So...that's it, they walk away?' I asked.

'Are you gonna tell your dad?' he asked.

'I haven't thought about it, I just assumed Roger and his pals would be arrested and everybody would know what he did.'

Jed stood up and went to the shed door to smoke his spliff. 'It's never that simple with guys like him.'

I took a deep breath and blew it out loudly.

'We'll send details and stills to freelancers and anyone else we think might give a fuck,' Jed said from the doorway. 'But be prepared, there aren't many heroes left these days.'

Rob and I just sat in silence, staring into space until Jed came back in. He gave a long sigh before squatting down by us. 'You're still so fucking innocent, aren't you?' he said. 'Haven't you ever heard of injunctions and D notices?' He put his hands on his head and pulled at his hair. 'Christ, is this what we're getting killed for?' His voice tailed off and he gathered us up, our heads close to his chest and he sobbed. Rob and I stared at each other. We didn't feel so innocent. When he pushed us away, he tousled our hair before walking out.

Rob nudged me. 'Anyway, you're free of Roger now, that's something.'

'It's not enough,' I said.

That evening the phone rang just as mam was getting the tea served.

'Ignore it,' dad said.

But I wasn't listening to him anymore; he brought Roger into my life. I picked up the phone.

'Channel 4 News — now!' Jed shouted.

Ignoring dad's threats, I went into the lounge and switched on the TV. Roger's face filled the screen. 'I'm resigning from the Shadow Cabinet and I'm resigning from my constituency,' he said.

Dad stopped shouting then; he just stood there with his mouth hanging open. The news reporter asked Roger why he was resigning at this time.

'Personal reasons, I'm not saying anything else,' Roger said as he pushed his way through the scrum.

I rang Rob's house, Jed picked up. 'Well?' he said.

'It's good but it's still not enough,' I said.

'You're right pal. He'll keep on doing it. He's got money, he's still a celeb of sorts and he's got friends in high places. But we made a difference. I'm off back to Helmund tomorrow. You and Rob look out for each other. Right?'

'Right.'

Dad sat on the sofa with his head in his hands. Mam leant on the draining board in the kitchen and poured herself a surreptitious gin. I blamed myself; I should never have got into his car a second time.

Noirish

GARY FIRST SAW HER ONE FRIDAY EVENING AT CENTRAL Library in the middle of the city. She was at the same crime novel event and sat next to him on the back row. She wore a black, fitted suit jacket over a pair of jeans and some chunky boots with a small heel. At one point she leaned over and whispered in Gary's ear.

'Great night isn't it?'

He noticed her spicy perfume and the way she sat so intently, taking everything in. As they queued to have their books signed, Ava engaged him in conversation.

'I haven't seen you at any of the other launches this autumn,' she said. Her eyes never left his face.

'I'm really only interested in crime,' he said as they moved closer to the front of the queue.

'Wow, that's cool,' she said. 'I've been collecting first edition crime novels for years now: Chandler, McDonald, Highsmith, Hammett, Thompson.'

'My favourites,' Gary replied.

Her dark glossy hair, crimson lips and easy laughter hit him below the belt. She was a perfect Noir heroine. Not a femme fatale but the type that had to be rescued by the hero who would be played by James Stewart, Humphrey Bogart or Gregory Peck. The thought galvanised him.

'Would you like to meet again?' he asked her as

they simultaneously reached the signing table.

She smiled, 'Yes, I would.' She touched his arm and let her hand linger longer than necessary.

They met in Tyneside Coffee Rooms, part of the Tyneside Cinema complex. It was Ava's suggestion and already one of Gary's regular haunts. He was a film and book buff with a special interest in Film Noir and when Ava started to talk about such classics as *The Third Man* and *The Maltese Falcon* his heart opened.

'Ava, you have a lovely way about you,' he said. 'It makes me feel at ease.'

She touched his hand. 'What a sweet thing to say; I feel really relaxed with you as well.'

'I've always been a bit awkward with women, especially beautiful ones like you.'

'I don't believe that, you're so charming,' she said and Gary's neck quivered to red-hot.

When she told him she'd recently been to a weekend Film Noir Festival in Copenhagen, he laughed.

'I don't believe it,' he said. 'I was there too. What did you see?'

'*Rear Window, The Long Goodbye, Double Indemnity*—' she said before he interrupted her.

'The third series of *The Killing*?' he asked.

'Of course, how did we miss one another?'

Gary flopped back in his chair. 'This is amazing,' he said. 'But I don't know how I didn't see you. We could have seen films together and talked all night long.'

'Good conversation is really delicious, like good food. Come on now; tell me who's your favourite noir male, on film?' she asked.

'Got to be Sam Spade as played by Bogart. Yours?'

'Well recently, Ripley as played by John Malkovitch.'

'Oh yes, I saw that film. He was magnificent; very close to the book, I thought. Though Matt Damon did a good job too.'

'Absolutely.'

Gary had never felt so snug with an attractive woman. Ava's obvious interest gave him confidence. In his late forties, he had almost given up hope of having a proper relationship.

'Where do you work?' he asked over their third cup of coffee.

'I'm freelance,' she said. 'Admin, accounts that sort of stuff. What do you do? No, wait, let me try and guess.' She looked him up and down, took his hands, turned them over and back before smiling. 'You don't work with your hands, manual stuff I mean. I think... you're a teacher of some sort, maybe further education?'

'Wow, how did you do that?' Gary asked. 'I teach English at one of the Durham Colleges. You'll be telling me my star sign next.'

Ava still held his hands. She looked at the palms, traced his lifeline with her finger and gazed into his expectant eyes. 'Virgo... and in Chinese Horoscopes, the Horse.'

Gary slapped the top of the table, nearly spilling both coffees. His laughter was so infectious that people stared at their table and smiled. Ava laughed with him and when they paid their bill and turned to leave, several strangers waved at them. It reminded him of so many scenes in his favourite films.

It drizzled as they walked to the metro station but nothing could stifle his spirit. They huddled under Ava's umbrella and then, as the train pulled away and he waved her off, he couldn't help thinking of *Brief Encounter*. Not strictly a noir film but so beautifully shot.

They saw one another every night for a week and parted at one metro station or another to go to their separate homes, his in Tynemouth, hers in Gateshead. On the seventh meeting, as they were putting on their coats at a Punjabi restaurant he said,

'Would you like to come back to my place?' He'd practised the words in front of his mirror the day before.

'And spend the night?' Ava asked.

Perhaps he'd been too bold.

'Well...I...yes...' he mumbled.

Ava grabbed his coat lapels, pulled him closer, reached up and kissed him.

They stayed in bed for most of the weekend, taking turns to make drinks or a bite to eat. Once he was over his embarrassment at Ava wanting the light on when they had sex, Gary was eager to try anything and she surprised him with her demands.

By Monday morning he was light headed. Small shivers furrowed his spine. His work colleagues noticed the difference. The most outspoken asked questions.

'What have you been up to Gary? A win on the pools?'

'No, he's finally discovered the pleasures of gin, haven't you?'

'It's a woman. Look at his eyes; they're orgasmic.'

Gary's only response was a small smile and a fragment from a Tina Turner song,

'*You're simply the best...better than all the rest... better than anyone, anyone I've ever met...*'

When he got home that evening Ava was still there. She'd made lasagne and a salad for his dinner. The flat was different. She'd moved things around, brought in some of her own furniture, ornaments and clothes. In the main bedroom the bed had been turned to face the window and billowing, flowery curtains replaced his neat wooden blinds. The changes made him uneasy. Since he left home, he'd never had to compromise with anyone over his living space.

'I hope you don't mind,' Ava said. 'You did give me a key and I thought if I was going to be staying here I might as well make it a bit more homely.'

'I...I think you should have asked me before moving stuff in,' Gary said.

Ava was aghast. 'Oh Gary, I'm sorry,' she said. Her hand flew up to her mouth and her eyes brimmed up. 'I'll move them all back out tomorrow.'

He folded his arms around her.

'It's all right. It's only a few things,' he said.

In bed later he forgot his doubts about what she'd done. Wasn't this what he'd been dreaming about: a partner with the same interests as himself and still young enough to have children? Relationships were about give and take, weren't they?

Next morning, before he left for work, he asked what she was cooking for dinner.

'Oh, I thought I told you. I'm going away for a few days. I'll phone you when I get back. And I'll move those things of mine out today. Everything will be back to normal when you come home tonight.'

Gary was thrown. He wanted to linger, to talk things through but he couldn't be late for work. Managers had to set a good example and there was that contract for a new waterfront swimming pool to go over. On the way to the office, he mulled over his time with Ava. His secretary noticed his distracted mood straight away.

'What's happened Mr Quinn? Have you had some bad news?' she asked.

He shook his head and shut himself in his room with the pool design plans and even ordered lunch in. The day dragged like never before. He texted Ava several times but there was no response. All day long a small part of him hoped that she would be waiting for him at home, with a chicken casserole bubbling in the oven and other delights promised for later on.

Ava wasn't at his place. The flat was empty and all the things she'd brought with her were gone. The place was cold and loneliness hit him like a wet sponge thrown by a heavyweight boxer. Standing at his window, he stared at the sea. It was charcoal grey, unfriendly and angry. Vigorous dogs crisscrossed the beach as if they were searching for something.

He went to bed early and was ambushed by Ava's

perfume on the pillows. He longed to feel her warm skin next to his, to hear her small chuckles as they made love.

Day by day his mood became gloomier. Every evening after work he went to Tyneside Coffee Rooms hoping to bump into her. A week later he was getting frantic. She'd said a few days so where was she? Had he driven her away with his selfish outburst? Why wasn't she responding to his texts? That afternoon the company chairman called him into his office.

'I don't know what's wrong with you Gary but whatever it is, it's damaging your work. I want you to take next week off and sort yourself out. Relax, tackle any problems head-on and come back refreshed. Several large contracts need settling by the end of the month and they belong to your department. Do you get my drift?'

'Yes, Mr Porter.'

Gary packed his briefcase and once more tried texting Ava. By the time he'd walked into the city and up to the third floor into Tyneside Coffee Rooms his mood had dived even further and he almost missed her. She was sitting in the farthest corner of the café reading a book. When he rushed up to her, he saw it was Dorothy Sayers' *Gaudy Nights*. She was dressed in black velvet with red boots that matched her lipstick. He wanted her so much he could barely speak.

He pulled out a chair and sat down, facing her. She looked embarrassed. He took hold of one of her hands. 'I've missed you so much,' he told her.

'I thought you wanted to back off...see other women, that you weren't ready for commitment.'

'No, it wasn't that. I was just a bit thrown. I've lived alone for a long time and I suppose I felt...sort of... invaded.'

She pulled her hand away and sighed. 'I'm sorry, Gary I got you wrong. I thought you were looking for a relationship, not just sex. I thought we'd found something special together.'

Her voice was hurt and she didn't look him in the

eye. He wanted the other Ava back. The one that laughed so much, licked his stomach and liked to share his bath.

'I'm the one that should apologise. I made a mistake. Ava, I do want a relationship with you. I want us to be together for...well, for as long as we love each other.'

She smiled and his juddering heart slowed down.

'You don't just want sex?'

'No, I want sex as well.'

Her laughter held promises for later.

'Well I don't want any more misunderstanding, so do you mind if I ask you some questions about your life and you can ask me anything you like?'

Gary nodded. His head was light, almost dizzy.

'Do you own or rent your flat?'

'I own it and I've just paid off the mortgage,' he proudly told her. 'What about you?'

'I rent. Does your family live close by?'

'Only my sister, she works out of Newcastle airport as cabin crew. My parents are quite elderly and live in Cornwall. You?'

'Just my mother and she lives in Gateshead too. Do you have any children?'

'No. What about you?'

She laughed. 'Not yet.'

He leaned over the table and kissed her. He wholeheartedly wanted her and that was enough for him.

Two nights later his sister, Milly met him from work and he told her about Ava.

'She's moved in already and brought some of her own furniture?' Milly said.

'Why shouldn't she? I want her to live with me. Wait until you meet her, you'll love her.'

'It's too soon. You don't know anything about her.'

'She's wonderful; you wouldn't believe how much we have in common. Come on, come back with me now.'

Milly went with him. Ava offered her shepherds'

pie and cabbage. She politely refused and went into the lounge.

'Darling you should have told me she was coming,' Ava whispered as they hid in the kitchen. 'I wanted everything to look fabulous for her first visit.'

Milly didn't stay long and as she was leaving she said to Gary,

'There's hardly room to turn around in the lounge and the spare bedroom is floor to ceiling with cardboard boxes. This is crazy, Gary.'

'It's my life, Milly. I don't tell you what to do,' he said.

'I'm worried.'

'Don't be, I'm having a lovely time.'

That night, Ava and he made love several times, in several different ways, in several different places and Gary fell into a contented sleep.

On Wednesday evening he returned home to a candlelit dinner of sweet and sour pork chops, roast potatoes and asparagus. Ava was stunning in a purple dress with a severely plunging neckline. He thought his heart might burst with pleasure. His own sofa was full of new bags and boxes, so after they'd eaten, they sat together on the single bed Ava had brought. She snuggled close to him and as they drank Cava, her hand rested on his thigh.

'Can you sign this before we go to bed?' she asked sweetly as she passed him an envelope.

Gary opened the folded sheets of paper and his breathing faltered. Ava had booked them in to be married at Newcastle Registry office on Saturday morning. He was speechless.

'You were going to make an honest women of me, weren't you?' She asked. Her face crumpled a little as she squeezed his hand.

'I...well...I...it's a little fast isn't it?' Gary said.

Ava was on her feet in an instant. Tears sparkled at the corners of her eyes.

'I thought we'd been through all this,' she said.

'We have...but—'

'Were you just planning on using and then dumping me?'

'No...no,' Gary said. He moved towards her and she backed away.

'Right, I'll have all my stuff out of here by the time you get back from work tomorrow. I'm sorry it turned out like this.' She ran to the bathroom and locked herself in.

Gary stood in the corridor listening to her sobs. He thought about life before Ava, how he'd craved for love. He remembered how he'd felt when she'd gone away. He thought about their lovemaking and her delicious cooking.

'Ava, I'm so sorry,' he said to the bathroom door. 'I want us to get married. It's just all been a bit sudden —'

A few seconds later she was out of the bathroom with her arms around his neck and her lips on his. They had sex on the floor in the corridor, his knees suffered minor burn marks from the carpet. Later, he signed everything and even gave her his credit card and PIN number so that she could buy a new dress for the wedding.

'Milly and my parents will be upset not to get an invite,' he said, later.

'My family too but it's our life darling. And... tomorrow night I've got a special treat for you; an authentic Mexican meal, while we watch *The Long Goodbye* on DVD.'

On Thursday afternoon he got a call from his bank.

'Mr Dinsdale, I'm afraid you've exceeded your credit card limit. We'd like you to come in and discuss the matter as soon as possible.'

Gary arranged an appointment, put the phone down and blew out a huge weary breath. But when he got home and saw the lovely meal, the wine, the popcorn and

Ava, dressed in a gorgeous vintage dress, he hadn't the will to upset her. He waited until after they'd eaten and watched the film.

'But darling,' she said, wide eyed. 'We are having a honeymoon aren't we? You said you'd take a week off work and I've booked us on the Orient Express, with a night in London before we leave and on the way back. The Savoy sweetheart, how noirish is that?'

She was so happy, he let it go. After all he had plenty of money in his savings account. She turned around and asked him to unzip her dress. He discovered she was naked underneath and he was lost in passion for well over an hour, until sleep caught up with him.

Friday, before leaving work he told everyone he was getting married the following day and they insisted on taking him out for a drink. They were all surprised at his speedy route to marriage. One or two of the older men took him to one side and hinted that he might be making a mistake. He smiled; they hadn't met Ava.

She was in the bath when he got home and from the front door she'd laid a trail of red rose petals for him to follow. There was a bottle of champagne in an ice bucket next to the bath. Ava had one glass in her hand and one on a tray, together with a box of his favourite dark chocolates.

'Get undressed very slowly,' she said.

The wedding ceremony was quick and efficient. The registrar took photos of them with Ava's new digital camera. She looked splendid in a vintage blue suit with a tight pencil skirt, high heels and a small velvet hat pinned on the side of her head. He wore his funeral gear, a dark three piece, with a white shirt and bow tie. They got a taxi to the Grand Hotel in Tynemouth where they'd booked an expensive lunch.

'To us darling,' Ava said, raising a champagne flute.

'To us,' he agreed.

Later, they drunkenly staggered along the seafront and back to his flat.

'Only one more day before our honeymoon,' Ava reminded him.

He grinned and passionately kissed her.

When they got to the flat there was a large removal van parked outside. Two men were carrying out his expensive double bed. A middle-aged woman, with a cigarette drooping from her bottom lip, followed them.

'Mum, come and meet Gary,' Ava shouted.

The woman ground out her cigarette on his immaculate lawn before waddling over to give him a nicotine kiss on his mouth. He pushed her away, held her at arm's length and stared at Ava.

'What the hell is going on?' he asked with a slight slur.

'Mum lives with me. I can't leave her to pay the rent in Gateshead all on her own, so she's moving in with us. She'll look after the place and my three cats while we're on honeymoon,' Ava beamed.

'But I don't like cats...and...and where's my bed going?'

'Everybody loves cats, you wait and see, oh and Mum and me always sleep in the same room because she has night terrors. We've put two single beds in the main bedroom.' She sidled up close to Gary and whispered, 'We can have sex anywhere. I'm looking forward to doing it on the beach.'

Gary suddenly imagined hundreds of grains of irritating sand in all his bits and pieces. He pushed past Ava's mother and the removal men to get to his flat. He would have shut and locked the door but Ava had a key. There was virtually nothing of his left in the place. A monster, wall-mounted flat screen with surround sound, had replaced his small TV. He snatched his mail out of the letter basket and locked himself in the bathroom. He put his head under the cold tap and drank several glasses of water. He took deep breaths and shouted as loud as he could, 'No...No...Nooooooooo.'

'Are you all right darling?' Ava asked through the gap in the door.

He didn't answer. Instead, he opened his mail. There was a red reminder about his subscription to Executive Dateline. He'd forgotten all about it. His new wife had told them he wouldn't be renewing and they wanted confirmation. They were delighted that the site had matched them so successfully and asked him for a personal endorsement.

He rang them on his mobile.

'Are you saying that Miss Ava Walters was also a member of Executive Dateline?' he asked.

'Yes sir.'

'She had access to my profile, everything about my likes and dislikes and what I'd done recently, like going to Copenhagen?'

'Yes sir.'

'But she didn't get in touch with me via the site?'

'She's a very romantic lady and wanted to arrange it herself. She was so sure you'd hit it off and she was right, wasn't she sir?'

Gary put the phone down. He opened the bathroom door.

'Ava?' he shouted.

'Yes, darling?'

'Who directed *The Third Man*?'

She manufactured a puzzled look. 'Sorry, I just can't remember his name.'

'Where was the Film Noir weekend held in Copenhagen?'

'Sorry, that's gone as well.'

'Who was Dashiell Hammet married to?'

She slowly shook her head.

'Get out of my flat, now.'

'Mum?' Ava called out. 'He's being horrible.'

Her mother waddled up the corridor.

'She's your wife, get used to it,' she said, lighting

up another tab. 'Take us to court if you don't like it. It'll take you at least six months to get us out of here, if you're lucky.' Then she put her arm around Ava and led her into the lounge.

That night Gary woke up and cracked his head on a brick wall. He was sleeping on a bench in Northumberland Park, inside a flimsy sleeping bag. It was well after midnight and the park was still and quiet. Gary began to make plans. First he would stop his credit card, then he would take his name off all the utility bills. It would be just like *The Maltese Falcon*, the 1941 version, where Brigid O'Shaughnessy couldn't believe that Sam Spade would actually turn her in to the cops. But he did in spite of his feelings for her. Now a *femme* had almost *fatally* wounded Gary... but he would have his revenge.

Armageddon

'WHAT ARE YOU DOING GRAN?' CAITLIN ASKED, ATTEMPTING TO keep the anxiety out of her voice. Since Granddad Lou had died, Caitlin's grandmother, Bridget, had been behaving strangely and the family were taking it in turns to visit and make sure she was coping.

Bridget's house overlooked the sea and usually everything was in the place it had been for a decade or more. Caitlin stared at all the objects lined up on the kitchen table.

'I'm getting prepared,' Bridget said.

'For what?' Caitlin asked.

'Armageddon.'

Caitlin didn't know what to say. Her eyes flickered over the wind-up head torch, wind-up radio, wind-up battery charger, first aid kit, painkillers, multiple use penknife, candles, lighters, small shovel, pens and notebooks.

'I've still got a few things to get.'

'Where did you get all this stuff from?'

'On the internet but I still need—'

Caitlin interrupted her. 'Gran, sit down and I'll make some tea.'

'There's not much time Caity. Didn't your mother pass on my message?'

'What message?'

Bridget Lisle took her granddaughter by the hands and sat her down on the settee. She put one arm around her shoulders and said,

'Last night your Granddad came to me in a dream and told me a Great Flood was on its way.'

Caitlin laughed. 'But it was only a dream gran, it's not real. You don't have to pack all this stuff, come on I'll help you—'

'No, you're wrong,' Bridget Lisle insisted. 'He came in a dream but then he stepped out and walked up to the side of the bed. He took hold of my hand and his skin was as warm as yours, though not so soft.'

'I'm sorry Gran but Granddad Lou's dead. It must have been a dream.' Caitlin stared at her grandmother. Tears tracked down the old woman's cheeks but her eyes were bright. 'It's all right Gran.' She gave her a hug and then said, 'I'm just going to phone Mam.'

'Use the landline.'

Caitlin shook her head. 'I'll go outside and ring her on the mobile. Won't be a minute.'

Bridget Lisle lived in a curved terrace of Victorian houses that traced the line of the bay below them. If you blinkered your eyes with your hands, there was nothing but sea for miles. Caitlin loved visiting; everything was so fresh, unlike the carbon air of the city where she worked, which made her eyes sting and her throat dusty. As she waited for her mother to answer the phone, she stared out at the sea. The tide was out, revealing all the hazardous rocks that had in the past scuppered so many boats. The ruins of one of them still lay beneath the water just beyond the bay and divers regularly came there as part of their training. The horizon seemed higher than she remembered. Was that possible? Did the horizon move?

'Hello Caity,' her mother said into her ear.

'Oh Mam, hi. Listen, why didn't you tell me about Gran's dream? She's up a height and packing things for survival.'

'What?'

'She says Armageddon's coming and the Great Flood's on its way.'

'Bloody hell, I thought she was just telling me about a dream. What's she packing?'

'She's got all sorts of wind-up stuff: radios, torches, battery chargers...you name it and she's got all her medication, food, the lot.'

'Have you asked her where she's going?'

'It wasn't the first thing that came to mind. She's really determined, I think you should come round.'

'It's Saturday, I'm having my hair done. Can you wait there till I've finished, just in case?'

'What time will you get here? I'm supposed to be meeting George in *The Salt House* for coffee.'

'Oh I see, three times in one week, sounds serious to me.'

'What time, Mam?'

'Just a minute, I'll check.'

Caitlin heard her mother's muffled voice talking to someone. She stared again at the horizon. One of the large ferries from Amsterdam was just coming into view; it would have to stand off until the tide was right. She checked her watch and noted that in about six hours it would pass the piers on its way to the dock. She decided she'd take George to see it in Tynemouth. It was worth the hike.

'Hello, Caitlin?'

'Yes?'

'I'll be another hour and then half an hour on the metro. Is that all right?'

'Oh my God.'

'Caitlin? What is it?'

'The ferry...it's disappeared.'

'You what?'

'The ferry, from Amsterdam; I saw it come over the horizon but now it's gone.'

She climbed up on the sea wall to get a better view.

'It's the light Caity; it plays tricks with your eyes. It'll be hidden by the swell. You'll see it again in a minute.'

'Mam, I know all about the light and the swells. It's a bloody great ferry, not a fishing boat and it's bloody gone.'

'Don't you start getting demented on me.'

'I'm telling you Mam, it's not there.'

'Listen sweetheart, Gran knows everything there is to know about the sea. She's only just stopped swimming in it every morning, hasn't she? Go and ask her to have a look-see then make her some tea and be nice to her.'

Swiping the hair out of her eyes Caitlin continued to stare at the horizon. Yes, it was windy and there was a swell on but not enough to obscure a massive ferry.

'Caitlin!' her mother shouted down the phone.

'Yes, I heard you. I'll stay with her till you come but hurry.'

Caitlin disconnected, jumped down off the wall and went back into her grandmother's house. She found her making a stack of sandwiches.

'Gran, come outside with me for a minute, will you?'

'What's wrong?'

'Just come and have a look.'

Bridget followed her out and Caitlin helped her on to the small wall. She pointed to where she'd last seen the ferry and told her what had happened. Her gran laughed.

'What?' Caitlin asked, miffed that she wasn't taking her seriously.

'I think what's happened is, because of the underwater hazards, the ferry's turned. You saw it sideways on but when it turns to front on it's so much smaller and what with the waves, the spray, the foam, it's difficult to make it out.'

Caitlin wasn't convinced; she didn't say so but she linked arms to go back inside the house and once they were in the kitchen, Caitlin said,

'Gran, sit down and listen to me, please.'

'I keep telling you; there isn't time. I've got to get packed and go to the lighthouse.'

'The lighthouse?'

'Yes, it's the only place around here built to withstand a raging flood and there's an old smuggler's tunnel underneath it that's been fortified as a nuclear bunker.'

'Gran, stop it.'

'Stop what?'

Caitlin swept her arm over all the objects on the table.

'This.'

'It's not a matter of choice, Caitlin; it's a necessity. How many times have I told you? We all belong to the sea.' She looked out of the window and sighed. 'Sometimes I can picture salty rust all over my body.'

Caitlin was used to her gran's obsession with the sea. She glanced around the kitchen and into the hall; the sea was everywhere: in pictures, photos, bits of driftwood, wall decorations, lighthouse chimes, seaweed patterns on the wallpaper, clear glass jars full of shells.

'Your Granddad always used to say, *the sea will take us all back one day and it will be a sweet and peaceful going.*'

Caitlin looked out at the ragged line of silver surf that always accompanied high tides. During one summer holiday when she was six, he and Grandma had taught her to swim, down in the bay. They were first in, screaming and throwing themselves under the waves, which seemed to her like mountains in motion. Slowly they encouraged her and their bull terrier, Tuppence, deeper and deeper. She watched them both, lying on the sea as if it were an enormous bed, rocking them up and down. And when she eventually learned how to lie back into the wings of the sea, she felt at peace.

'The best thing you can do, Caitlin, is go to your

flat, pack a bag, get your mother to do the same and then come and pick me up. We can't do anything for your brother Tom but it's very high up in Afghanistan so he might be fine. I'll have flasks and water and sandwiches ready for all of us.'

'What if Mam and me don't believe you?'

'That's your look out but you'll be making a big mistake and I'll go without you if I have to; I'll get a taxi.'

Caitlin decided to try logic. Sometimes confused minds had a kind of logic to what they said and did. 'Gran, if there is a great flood coming and me and Mam and everybody else you know is going to die, because they don't believe it, why would you want to survive?'

'Haven't you ever read the bible?'

Caitlin shook her head. She'd never seen her grandmother reading it either.

Bridget Lisle stopped doing the sandwiches and sat down. 'After Armageddon, the dead will all rise up for the Day of Judgement and that means me and Granddad Lou will be together again.'

Before Caitlin could respond, her mobile rang. It was her mother calling. She went outside where the signal was better.

'Yes, Mam.'

'I've been talking to your Aunty Ivy. She says that if Grandma's got dementia or Alzheimer's you mustn't argue with her because it just confuses them even more.'

'Oh, bugger.'

'What?'

'I've been trying to reason with her but it's not making any difference.'

'Well try agreeing with her and see what happens. I'll be there soon and Ivy's coming straight after her shift at the hospital.'

Caitlin stood outside for a while. The tide had turned and the sea was gathering momentum but there was still no sign of the Amsterdam ferry. She was worried and wasn't ready to lose gran to some cruel disease.

In the kitchen, Gran was filling four flasks with coffee and had a pot of tea on the go. She pushed a mug towards Caitlin. 'There you are pet, just how you like it,' she said.

Caitlin sat at the table and snared a couple of Rich Tea biscuits to dunk. She watched her Grandma fiddling with the flasks and sipping her tea and listened as she sang softly a song they'd played at Granddad's funeral, *The Water of Tyne:*

> *I cannot get to my love if I would dee*
> *For the water of Tyne run between him and me*
> *And here I maun stand wi a tear in my eye*
> *All sighin and sobbin my true love to see*

She looked happy, even content and Caitlin hadn't seen her like that since Granddad Lou went downhill.

'You miss him, don't you Gran?'

She nodded and blew her a kiss.

'Tell me how you know about the secret tunnel and the nuclear bunker.'

Bridget Lisle looked thoughtfully at her.

'When he was a lad, Lou was involved in a bit of smuggling. It was during the war and they kept some of the stores in that tunnel. Seems there was only half a dozen of them knew about it. All but one them's dead and the one that's left's in a nursing home.'

'What about the nuclear part? Granddad and his mates wouldn't know how to do that?'

'Davy Freeman did. He was an engineer at that place in West Cumbria...'

'Sellafield?'

'It was called Windscale then. Anyhow he was sent to help create a nuclear bunker somewhere near Carlisle and he copied the engineering plans and even kept some of the leftover materials.'

'Why?'

'He always said: *what's good enough for them is good enough for us*. Ban the Bomb was a big thing then.

We all thought some daft bugger would press a button.
When Davy retired back over here, him and the lads
turned the smuggling cave into a bunker and each of the
men's families had a set of keys.'

She took them out of her pocket and showed
them to Caitlin.

'I've never seen keys like that.'

'There's two codes as well. I've got them written
down but we've got to get to the lighthouse before it
closes.' She checked her watch. 'Tide's turned and it'll
come in quickly, we've not got much time.' She took hold
of Caitlin's hand. 'Do you believe me now?' She asked.
Caitlin nodded, as her mother had told her to do. 'Then
start loading this lot into your car and ring your Mam and
tell her to us to meet there. She'll have to miss out on her
blow dry.'

Caitlin turned the TV on to a news channel. She
hoped that seeing everything was normal on the telly
might trigger a bit of sanity in her Gran. Then she went
outside to phone her Mam, who was under a dryer.

'Mam, you've got to meet us at the lighthouse
before the tide covers the causeway otherwise it'll be too
late.'

'But mi hair...'

'It'll be ruined in the flood anyway.'

'Have you gone mad?'

'You told me to go along with Gran. Get a move
on.'

While her Gran got into some warmer clothes,
Caitlin loaded up her small 4 x 4. She watched two dogs
leaping into the waves in the bay below, both Cumberland
terriers. They barked with delight. But all at once they
stopped on the beach, ears high and swivelling. They
ignored the sticks being thrown for them. Caitlin listened
too. She stared at the horizon and to the south.
Sometimes you could see a plane coming up the coast
before you could hear it. As she watched she heard a low
rumble and a few seconds later a chunk of rock about six

feet wide fell away from the headland on Marconi Point. The dogs started barking again and ran off the beach and up the slope, chased by their confused owners.

When she climbed down off the wall, her Gran was standing nearby looking out to sea wearing her best woollen coat with the fur collar.

'You look smart, Gran.'

'You saw that cliff fall didn't you? It's time to go,' she said and then she pointed, 'and there, look, the Amsterdam ferry's turning again.'

Caitlin sighed, her Gran had been right all along. She helped her into the jeep and turned the radio on. As they drove along the coast towards the lighthouse, a newsflash blared out.

We interrupt this programme with a warning for all coastal areas and all sea traffic around the British Isles, most especially in the North S ea, the North East and East. A severe quake has been detected off the coast of Sweden. First thoughts are that, due to the tremors, a submerged piece of coastal Sweden, below Bergen, has been separated from the mainland and is now a dangerous hazard. It is the size of a large iceberg but with most of its landmass beneath the water. All shipping vessels are warned to operate on radar and turn on the emergency frequency. All residents should stay away from beaches and cliffs overlooking the sea. Emergency Services have been informed. Some residents will have to be evacuated. More news as we receive it.

'This is the start,' Bridget Lisle whispered. 'All them greedy oil companies, scrabbling about and drilling for oil and gas in the Arctic. It's reckless; there's no proper safety precautions and they don't understand the sea.'

Caitlin glanced at her Grandma. 'How could you know about all this, Gran?'

'I told you. Lou came and warned me. He told me to look on the internet and I did. Can't you go any faster?'

Caitlin accelerated. The lighthouse was up ahead

and as they approached the turn into the small road, she saw blue police lights flashing in her rear view mirror. She put her foot down and took the corner at forty, almost losing control. The road was full of cars driving away from the island. Caitlin had to mount the kerb on the wrong side of the road to get past them. In her mirror she saw police vehicles setting up a roadblock and she guessed she'd probably have to drive off road and across the golf course if she wanted to make a quick escape.

She pulled up at the bottom of the slope at the start of the causeway to the island, which was still water free.

'You'll have to drive over; it'll take too long to carry all this stuff.'

'But—'

'No buts darling.'

Catlin drove slowly across the causeway. Behind her, people were shouting and at the end of the causeway they signalled for her to go back. She ignored them all and when she got to the other side, pushed through them to get to the back of the vehicle. People shouted at her,

'What are you doing?'

'Haven't you heard the news?'

'The tide's coming in.'

A man in a North Tyneside Council sweatshirt took hold of her arm as she attempted to unload the vehicle.

'You can't park here. You haven't got a permit,' he said.

Caitlin started laughing. 'Bugger off, this is an emergency,' she said.

'We've already got an emergency and we're evacuating the island.'

Bridget Lisle walked round the vehicle and nudged his arm. 'Stephen Sheridan, make yourself useful and help Caitlin.'

'Mrs Lisle...I...I'

'Just do it or I'll tell your nana you insulted me.'

All the knowledge of lives spent pulling herring, mending nets, snapping prawns, selling fish door to door, swept through Stephen Sheridan's mind and nana-power won the day. Within five minutes everything was unloaded and carried to the door into the lighthouse shop.

'I'll go and get Mam,' Caitlin said to her gran.

'Give us a hug, just in case.'

As they fiercely embraced, Stephen Sheridan stood shyly, waiting.

'Oooh, I do love you, Gran.'

'I know and now hop it.'

'Mrs Lisle, you can't stay here. It's dangerous, they're clearing the whole place,' Stephen Sheridan said.

'They'll have to find me first,' she said.

'I'll be back as soon as I find Mam,' Caitlin told her.

'They won't let anyone come over,' Stephen said, trying hard to do his job.

As Caitlin drove back, the sea was just creeping over the edges of the causeway. She took it very slowly. Several policemen stood waiting on the mainland. As she drew level with them, one came over to her driver's window. She opened it to hear what he had to say.

'Please drive slowly down to the main road.'

'I don't want to leave. I've just come to pick up my Mam and take her over to the island.'

'You can't do that. We're evacuating the island and all this area.'

Through her mirror she could see Stephen Sheridan leading a dozen people along the causeway. She got out of the car and searched for her Gran and saw her standing on the wall surrounding the lighthouse, waving. There was a strange light around her, as if she was hovering above the wall. Two policemen ran on to the causeway to hurry people along; the sea was splashing round their ankles.

'Miss? Please move your vehicle now or one of my

officers will have to drive it away.'

Caitlin looked round to see a high-ranking police officer. And behind him, with her hair still in rollers, her mother barging her way forward, swatting anyone who tried to stop her. Caitlin got out of the car and gave the keys to the officer. Her Mam flew into her arms as two constables tried to grab her.

'Did you get across? Where's Gran?' She asked breathlessly.

'She's over there, standing on top of the bloody wall.'

They both let out a nervous laugh.

The officer with Caitlin's keys passed them on, with orders to shift the car. He then said something to another officer and several constables began moving.

'Come on then, we can't leave her there on her own,' said Caitlin's mother.

The two women joined hands but as they started to move forward, several policemen overtook them and formed a wall across the causeway.

'Nobody is going over to the island,' said the high rank.

'But my Gran's on the island,' Caitlin said.

'Yes and you drove her there and now two of my men will have to risk their lives to go and fetch her back.'

'She won't come,' Caitlin said but it was too late, the policemen were on their way and she and her mother were bustled up the slope towards a police van. Sitting in the van, high up in the car park, they couldn't see any sign of Bridget. The policemen were almost halfway across the causeway and the sea was licking the top of their wellies.

Suddenly they turned and ran back towards the mainland. Voices shouted and people ran up towards the main road, cars screeched out of the car park. Caitlin and her mother got out of the van just in time to see an enormous swell building up beyond the lighthouse. It was moving at great speed and rising as it came. Several policemen tried to grab them and push them back into the van but they hugged each other and refused to move.

As people took off in every direction, the police van was abandoned. Caitlin and her mother watched as the wave grew and grew until it was as tall as the lighthouse. It seemed to hover in the air for a moment until it crashed down on the island with a noise like an explosion and the enormous sea hurtled towards the mainland.

Caitlin and her mam were speechless. She opened the van door and saw the keys in the ignition.

'Quick, jump in the back!' she shouted as she started the engine.

As soon as her mam's feet hit the van floor, Caitlin put her foot down.

'Hold tight and leave the back doors open, mam, we'll pick up any stragglers.'

In the driving mirror Caitlin could see the crashing water hurtling along behind her. She slowed to let several police constables jump in and climbed the pavement to pass abandoned vehicles.

'What's the highest spot near here?' she shouted out as she approached the main road. She saw her jeep abandoned by the cemetery and her heart tumbled; it had been a fantastic jalopy.

'Seaton Sluice roundabout then left towards Earsdon,' a woman shouted.

The road was clear as she swung the van round and after the sharp bend put her foot to the floor and raced up the hill. To her right she saw that the sea had swallowed the big car park and was heading across the fields towards them. Everyone in the back of the van was silent. They knew she was going as fast as she could.

'It's a risk taking the first turn to Earsdon because the road dips wildly before rising again,' a man shouted.

'But if we go straight over the roundabout we'll be going parallel to the sea and we can't outrun it,' another voice shouted.

Caitlin hit the roundabout at fifty miles an hour.

She braked hard and almost mounted the kerb as she took the left turn. In her mirror the sea was hurtling up the bridleway towards the Seaton Delaval Arms. She almost pushed the accelerator pedal through the van floor.

'Hold on,' she shouted. She had to get to the uphill section before the sea caught up with them. She didn't expect anyone to be on the road so she took the bends wide and too fast. Just as she began climbing the hill, the sea appeared in her mirror. She changed down to second gear and gunned the engine upwards. As they got near the top, the water hit the rear van doors and helped move it forward. But as the van engine screamed and then started roller-coastering downwards, the water ran out of steam and only a shallow stream rose over the wheels.

Everyone watched as the sea began retreating at an amazing speed.

'Me and Mam are going back to the island,' Caitlin said as she manoeuvered a five point turn on the narrow road. Everyone except her mother left the van and she joined Caitlin in the front.

'How far do you think it'll go back?' Caitlin asked. Her mother was busy pulling out her rollers and running her fingers through her hair.

'Not a clue,' her mother said. 'D'you think she got to the bunker?'

'I'm not sure she ever intended to.'

'What d'you mean?'

'I think she just wanted to be with Granddad Lou. The lighthouse stuff was just to distract us, she knew we'd never get back across to the island and she didn't want us to try and stop her.'

Her mother choked up. 'That's where Dad proposed to her, at the top of the lighthouse,' she said.

'We'll never see her again,' Caitlin said.

'Don't say that. But...I think you're probably right; it's what she wanted. She found out about the underwater disturbance and the potential freak wave and took it as a sign.'

The road was littered with abandoned vehicles and bicycles. Some of buildings had been damaged and lots of dazed people were walking about. There were sewage, pans, boxes and all sorts of litter in the streets. Ambulances, fire engines and police cars were everywhere, trying to help the walking wounded and being assisted to carry others on stretchers.

'She was right about the great flood,' Caitlin said as they crawled along, more stop than go.

'I was just thinking that.'

The road to the island was blocked. They left the van and went along the cliff tops. The police couldn't be everywhere. The water had receded to the level of a very high tide. There'd be no crossing the causeway for hours. The lighthouse had withstood the attack quite well. Only the very top was actually missing.

'It'll be full of water won't it? Caitlin said.

'Who knows?'

'Let's go to Gran's, see how her place got on.'

They drove in silence but as they approached Whitley Bay they saw that no freak wave had hit the coast there or in Cullercoats. Caitlin turned on the radio.

... And it appears to be confined to one small area of the North East coast, the newscaster said.

'Bloody Hell,' her mother shouted.

Bridget Lisle's terrace was still standing but the path to it was like a shallow stream. The tide had risen higher than ever before recorded. The residents stood around in little groups, too stunned to speak.

Caitlin opened her Gran's door; there was no damage, not even a trickle of water. Not a drop had penetrated the house. They went into the kitchen, the centre of the house. The interior seemed to be full of static, the atmosphere was dense and the light sharp, like pre-storm brilliance. Caitlin heard the thrum of their heartbeats.

On the table, an envelope was propped against the sauce bottle. Caitlin picked it up just as heavy rain began drumming on the windows and roof. She turned the envelope over in her hands. It was her Gran's writing, neat italic script.

'Don't open it,' her mother said.

'It's got my name on it.'

'The envelope's sealed, there's no harm in waiting, is there?'

Caitlin hesitated; her mother was behaving out of character. And then it clicked; it could be her G ran's suicide note. She put the envelope back and almost immediately, the sound of laughter and cheering filtered in from outside and the rain stopped. They ran to the door and into the garden. An enormous double rainbow stretched from one side of the bay to the other. Caitlin's mother took hold of her hand.

'Say goodbye,' she said.

'Goodbye Gran, safe journey.'

Caitlin closed her eyes and on the inside of her lids she saw her Gran and Granddad swimming in their seal skins beneath the sea; their movements were sleek and iridescent.

Caged

THEY LIVE ON THE STREET; NO, THEY LIVE IN CAGES ON THE
street, where the smells are harsh acid and they're close
to traffic fumes and a terrible, inexorable dust. Day and
night the noise is relentless; horns, hooters, voices
shouting, arguing, laughing and begging. These girls are
goods for sale, just like all the other things on the street.
People pause and stare as they would at animals. A young
man, who's seen your camcorder, approaches.

'You journalist? You want story? Exclusive? You
pay me?'

He takes you to a nearby holding prison. You
watch him talk to the guard and wonder if you should run
back into the safety of the crowds. Returning, the young
man says,

'Show me money.' When you do, he takes five
dollars for himself and five for the guard, who beckons
you inside the metal door. Five dollars is very little
money. He saw you had much more but he only took what
he thought was fair. What bizarre logic so close to a street
where children are sold for sex.

'She is Rajinder; she speak English,' the boy says
before he leaves.

You follow the guard through a dark, damp
corridor. Underfoot the ground is rutted. You stumble,
put your hand on the wall; it slides on slime and you

almost fall. The guard turns and laughs, his rancid breath
rushes at you. He unlocks a metal door and lets you into a
cell.

She's alone in a room the size of a small toilet.
There's just enough space for her to lie flat but her head
and feet butt up against the walls. There's one scabby
blanket. Two buckets stand in the corner. A plank of wood
sits on top of them but doesn't fully cover the openings.
The smell is sulphuric; it catches in your nose and throat.
It's the only place to sit. You tell Rajinder you want to
hear her story.

'Why you want to know these things from me?'
she says. 'You can ask any other.' The guard shouts at her.
'Ah, you have paid him for time, like a man does... and
maybe he gives me extra rice tonight...yes, you can use
your recording machine.'

The guard still stands there with the door open.
You stare at him until he shrugs, locks the door and
leaves. You ask her how long she's been for sale.

'Too many years. Men with money and machetes
took me from my village and it is so hard to keep my
home in my mind. Papa said I must go with them. Mama
promised to come. *Remember,* she told me, *you are
working for all of the family. Money will be sent back to
us and we will pray for you and offer blessings.*'

Her eyes turn still and blank. She's learned not to
feel. You can't imagine what that's like. You have to resist
the urge to pull her into your arms. There are dozens and
dozens of young women like her and because they're sold
into this modern slavery to make money for their
families, nobody helps them.

'Yes, I was virgin,' she replies to your question. 'I
did not know a man before and when the first one came
to me I set to screaming and crying as he tried to push his
meat inside me. He was the lover of Maman; mistress of
our cages and her gift to him is to break our virginity. She
helped him, holding me in her fat arms and spreading oily
cream into my bleeding place. I cried three full nights,

while all about me men grunted and sighed and push-pushed their meat into other girls as young as me and older.'

'Did none of them help you?' you ask.

'How could they help? We are in separate cages. The doors are not left open when the men come. If you want to pee there is the bucket, emptied by Jasmine twice a day. For back passage stuff we must shout to be taken to the shed behind the buildings. Every day we have full body wash and a wet rub down below, between men.'

You ask how old she is and who is the oldest one in the cages. A second later you wish you hadn't.

'None grow old in this place,' she says. 'At sixteen we are no further interest to these men with skins of all colours and voices from around the world. They are rough with us, like we are to blame for them wanting us. And after, when they are leaving and we are covered in bruises and their pungent juices, stinking and sometimes sobbing, they do not meet our eyes. What does this mean?'

There's no easy answer to her question. You're a young trainee reporter on a regional newspaper. You're on a month's holiday with your parents. They don't know you're here. While they take in the sights, they think you're in the hotel swimming pool, or on the sun terrace with your iPad.

'If a man wants, he can take a girl away for up to one year, even to other countries, to be shared out like rice from a pan. Many go to other lands and never come back. Maman takes big deposits on these girls; she knows they will not all return. Some do, almost dead and soaked with disease. Then maman will not keep them, they are sent back to their villages to die. They could tell you of the horror, what some men will do for their own pleasure; men who pretend to the world to be holy and good.'

You ask about her English, where she learned it.

'Maman teaches us to speak English. She says the men like us to speak dirty words to them; they will pay more for this. Some girls taught me dirty words from other lands: German, Italian, Spanish, French, Russian, Arabic, Jewish, Polish, Japanese, Dutch, even from places I never heard about. The more you earn the happier you make Maman. An angry Maman is sometimes as bad as the men. It is to be avoided.'

The guard shouts, you must leave or pay more money. You can't stand the smell any longer. You tell her you'll see her the next day. She nods slowly. She knows not to trust anyone. You ask if there's anything you can get for her.

'A Mars Bar?' she asks.

You sleep badly. Even hot milk and honey is useless. In the early hours you bump into your mother in the bathroom. She senses something different about you. As she touches your shoulder, her eyes seek answers. You smile and shake your head. She asks you to accompany her on the following day's outing. Your father has his heart set on a museum in the city but she wants to go to the hills to a holy ruin. You shake your head again and in your room, toss and turn until dawn. You want to kill the men who use these girls. What makes men like that you ask yourself, men from all corners of the world?

Next day you take Rajinder fruit and Mars Bars. She thanks you and eats with small bites to savour the taste. Before leaving the hotel you rubbed lavender oil above your top lip to help with the stench. She tells you more about her Maman.

'In quiet times, Maman told us of her own arranged marriage, to a man born here but living in Glasgow, Scot L and. She was sent to marry him at fifteen and when she got there he had a white wife kept in secret and wanted Maman only for children. Lies, beatings and making her watch him with his white lover, drove Maman near to crazy. He told her she must keep his secrets, or she would destroy his honour and he would kill her. She ran away and was helped by some white whores, doing

tricks at railways and ports. After weeks she found ship
passage home and food in return for giving her body to
the crew. She lost one baby and became pregnant with
one other on that hellish journey and her baby, Jasmine
was born on streets nearby.

Another Maman took her and Jasmine in and it
nearly sent our Maman crazy wild to know that full-
grown men were having her baby for their filthy desires.
That is when she swore to make her own caged whore
place, where no child before eleven years old would be
used and abused and all her girls would be on pills to stop
them becoming with child. Outside she advertises this
and also that men must use the free condoms she
provides. Jasmine is grown now but her eyes are turned
back into her head for what she has seen and been
through, and she has no words.'

So little in her story relates to your experience, it
feels like you're living a dream or more specifically, a
nightmare. A large part of you wants to run away, never
come back to this place of horror that you stumbled into.
Another part knows that you will write a good feature on
it, that a national paper will pick it up. You ask Rajinder if
you can take a photograph of her. Her smile is knowing,
she sees through you. She sees who you are. She asks for
money. You give it to her; she hides it under her blanket.
You ask more about her family, does she have brothers
and sisters?

'My young sister, Sunita was married to the god,
Jamdagmi and became devadasi, whore to god. You know
of this god?'

You tell her you don't know of this god tradition
but would like to.

'Jamdagmi is husband to the goddess, Yellamma.
Long time back, the devadasis were celibate: sworn to
never have sex and be pure handmaidens, guarding
temples. Not so now; priests marry girls to Jamdagmi so
that rich men can use them. Sunita went at eleven years,
just as I came here. When the priest had married her she

was taken to a rich man's house for his pleasure. I remember Mama giving her a red cloth and telling her to bite on it when the pain came and not to let out any cries. Girls are sometimes given up to the priests in the hope that god will give them some boy children. Mama and Papa got one sack of rice and a sickly goat in exchange for Sunita.'

Rajinder turns away from you. She doesn't want you to see her cry. You're not worthy of that. One sack of rice and a sickly goat, you repeat the phrase inside your head: the going rate for a child's innocence.

'I think of Sunita and my village, some dark nights,' Rajinder continues.

It's as if she now wants the story told.

'Even though food was short there and enemies with guns and knives sometimes attacked our village, I would be there if I could. There was a special, sweet smell at waking times, made by some sort of gum tree, Papa said and I would have it in my nostrils before my eyes opened to the sun. Our village had many trees around it, welcome shade from the careless heat, and sandy places to play and run. And as was the custom, Papa would listen to all our dreams at morning and take them to the meeting of elders for discussion about how the omens lay. It wasn't until after the second drought, when the riverbed was so dusty even the elephants stayed away, that girls and boys from our village were sold to the city men.'

You ask if she is angry about what has happened to her and her sister, Sunita.

'Yes, angry... full of rage; you know that. Sometimes I attacked men who hurt me, bit them and scratched their faces so someone might notice. But nobody wants to know. Nobody cares; like those dying of starvation on the streets, while others eat to bulging fatness. We are hidden from tourists...except those who come for sex with us. Men from your country? Yes of course, many, old men and young. Some Mamans along

the street sell amputee or disabled children. This is
something many men from your lands want.'

It beggars belief. Your skin begins to goose up
and you find it hard to breathe. You didn't think you were
naïve but now you know you are.

'Sometimes I would dream of going over the sea
to a place with plenty water and cool breezes. I'd make an
escape, ask someone to help. But Maman told me that
death is the only escape. In all the countries where men
took her girls for sex, they were hidden, used in secret
and never seen by other people, who might have cared,
just a little. When I heard some of what happened to
Sunita, messages that came with other girls sent here, I
lost my desire to live.'

You want to hear but you don't want to hear. You
justify it to yourself: it's your duty to let the world know
what is happening. Of course, that's what journalists do.

'She was kept in one room with a patch of earth
outside and a wash and toilet cupboard. It was at the edge
of the man's big estate and he would come to her often...
until she was pregnant for the second time. She lost the
first baby because the man beat her up when he found she
was with child. This second time he threw her out with
just the clothes she was wearing. I think she was picked
up from the roadside by another, poorer man who kept
her in a shack but he let her have the baby and it was a
boy, who he took away as his son. That is all I know.'

'Do I wonder about this life? It is not a life, miss;
it is Hell. I have no life since eleven years old. I am now
fifteen and I am a shell that no sea has sung in. Even the
make-up Maman gives us cannot keep me looking young
for much longer. We are shrivelled souls... and that is why
I did it.'

She looks at me from under her sparse eyelashes;
her face has a hunted quality.

'That's what you really want to know, isn't it?
That's why you're here? You want to know why I cut his
throat with Sanjat's open razor?'

You ask who Sanjat is.

'Sanjat is the transvestite whore who lives above my cage. He is my friend. He was shaving the hairs from his body ready for a nightlong customer when he heard my screaming. He ran to me with the razor still in his hand. This man had bitten chunks of flesh from my breasts and was forcing his meat into my mouth. I kicked him off and stamped hard in his balls. When Sanjat got the door open and rushed in, I pulled the razor from his hand and slit the man ear to ear.'

'What will happen? I will soon die. Better that than be thrown on the street by Maman and be used by everybody for free until a slow death in some stinking gutter. The guard has already beaten me and will do so again. He sells me too. Did you know that?'

You shake your head, look towards the guard. He's looking through the bars, and leers. He's in control. You have to get out of the fetid place. You feel impotent, enraged with the men who use these women and with the women who herd them into cages. This land, it has so much beauty and history and so much horror side by side. That's what you will write about. It will make a difference; it has to. You ask Rajinder if you can take another photo.

'What else you have in your bag except money?' She whispers. Like a claw, her hand grips mine. 'Scissors? A knife? Matches? Something I can use to end this life of horror? You must help me.'

Putting your back to the guard, you search your bag. You move closer to the girl and pass her a pair of small but sharp nail scissors. The guard shouts, tells you to stay back from the girl. You hear the fear in his voice. Two women are conspiring. Two women are stronger than one.

You take her photo, tell her how beautiful she still looks. She knows you are lying. You turn off your camcorder, say goodbye to the girl, and thank her.

'Pray for me,' she says. You nod, knowing you have no intention of praying. Any God who allows the

horror Rajinder has seen and heard to continue, is no
God you want to know.

Outside, the air is thick with dust and oil.
Garbage lingers on every corner. You walk slowly down to
the street where you first met the youth. You take photos
of the children in the cages, of the signs advertising very
young children, even photos of naked babies. You start to
gag, wish you had gone into the hills with your mother or
to the museum with your father. And just as you turn
away you see him, coming out of the house Rajinder
mentioned, the house of caged, amputee children. He
looks pleased with himself. He brushes himself down,
smoothes back his hair, turns towards the city: your
father, the surgeon. You gasp, hand to your mouth, heart
squeezed by unseen hands. As he turns to flag down a
taxi, you lift your camera and take his photo.